# White Snow

# and the Mountain

# Spirit

# Chapter 1

The sky is bright white, not a patch of blue can be seen. The fluffy clouds above threatening snow with every passing minute. Arella pulls her cloak tighter, the winter chill biting at her face. "It's gotten really cold really fast." She stutters a little. "It won't be long before the snow starts to fall."

"Well we are climbing a mountain Arella." Nootau laughs.

"Sort of yeah, although it doesn't really feel like we're going up hill much yet." Arella contests. The ground around them sloped up for a while from where they camped next to the canyon, but soon evened out again. It has become clear that it will take longer than they first anticipated to reach the peak of the mountain.

"Maybe we should find somewhere to camp soon." Nashoba says. Just as he speaks, a small white flake falls from the sky. "There is snow on it's way, and we shouldn't be caught out in it unprepared. Arella do we have any food?"

"Not yet we don't" She steps forwards. "Me and Maska will find some food then meet you back at camp."

"How will you know where we are camped?" Mato asks, the scar on his face pulling up with his eyebrow in question. "We haven't chosen anywhere yet."

"Come on Mato, I'm sure Maska can sniff you guys out wherever you go." She laughs, and so do the others. Nashoba brings her attention to a rocky wall.

"I'm sure there'll be a cave around here somewhere." He says, looking serious. "We'll find a safe place to camp and firewood, you take care of the food"

Arella and Maska turn to head deeper into the pine trees, on the hunt for food for them and the men to eat. The trees that grow here and thin and tall. They have leaves, but not many of them. It is a strange place they have come to, and they wonder what they will find at the top of the mountain. Letting Maska lead the way, following the scent of some sort of animal, Arella begins to think, letting her mind wander. Nashoba has been strange with her. He's always strange, but he's being even stranger now. It's like he's two different people. When they are alone he is sweet and gentle, he tells her she is the most beautiful thing he has ever seen, and that he could stay with her, staring into her violet eyes forever. Arella loves this Nashoba, although she would not say it to him, she dare not speak the words. However, when They are with the others, Nashoba is the opposite. He will not look her in the eye, will not speak directly to her, and pays her very little attention. She's been meaning to bring this up with him, but every time she tries, they are either interrupted, or she is too lost in the green fields that are his eyes. *"I wonder if he does actually like me?"* This thought has passed through her mind so many times since the night at the lake, the first time Nashoba kissed her.

Maska breaks Arella out of her thoughts by nudging her. She instinctively gets down low to the ground. The grunting ahead suggests that boar is on the menu tonight. She hears it before seeing the creature, and Maska sniffed it out. Arella breathes deep, catching the musky scent of the boar in her nostrils, the chill biting at her as she breathes in. She pulls her fur hood up over her head, pulls her bow from her back and knocks an arrow. She turns to look at Maska, nodding to let him know she is ready to hunt. He blinks his strange eyes at her, the green and yellow shining in the dim light. He steps forwards, slowly, crouched low to the ground. He moves around to the left, intending to flank the boar. She moves a little to the right, knowing Maska will flush the boar towards her. She moves to a position behind a narrow tree, taking aim at the boar.

The black pig snuffles in the mud, searching with white tusks, looking for foots in the hard ground. The temperature here has frozen the ground, making it hard for most animals to survive. The winter has hit here first, at the foot of the mountain, halting the growth of any plants that might have grown here before. The only creatures left now are those who can dig through the frozen ground, those who hibernate, or the ones who eat the others.

Maska creeps forwards, keeping both eyes on the boar between them. He peeks up at Arella, who knocks an arrow on her purple bow. She pulls back, ready to fire if Maska misses his prey. The black cat steps forwards on delicate paws, careful not to crunch the cold dry ground beneath his feet. He extends his claws, readying for the pounce. Just as Maska leaps forwards, the boar catches scent of him. It squeals and dives to the side. Maska just misses, landing on the hard ground face first. "I got it!" Arella shouts, pulling her arrow back as far as her arms can draw. She lets loose the bloodglass arrow, hitting the boar on the kind flank. Maska quickly regains footing and lunges for the boar, landing hard on its back, killing it quickly with his sharp teeth. "Nice moves." Arella praises. The auron cat bristles at her compliment.

After hauling the dead boar onto her shoulder, Arella and Maska set off back to the caves where they left the men. It doesn't take them long to reach the spot where they left them, and soon Maska picks up their trail. The follow the scent the auron cat has picked up to an area where the caves get bigger. Soon, Arella even knows where they are. Wispy smoke rises from the entrance of one of the caves, the inside lit up in a dim orangey glow."*Warmth, finally*". It is getting colder the further up the mountains they travel, and the night-time fires are a blessing.

Light laughter can be heard from the cave entrance. Maska is first to enter, he walks in proudly, his head held high. Arella follows soon after, a smile on her pale face, the freshly killed boar over her shoulder. "I can't believe you two catch boar on your own." Nootau laughs. "Me and Nashoba barely managed it when we last tried."

"I remember that day very clearly." Arella laughs, then her face changes. "Not such a great day on the whole really was it?"

"Not really." Mato answers.

"Brought us all together though." Arella says.

"That's true." Nootau replies. Arella drops the boar to the ground. Mato begins preparing it for cooking. He's gotten fairly good at this recently. Arella looks around the cave they're chosen as their bed for the night. It is fairly small, with a low roof, but just big enough for them all to squeeze in. The entrance is fairly small, but it widens out just inside, making a nice place to spend the night. The fire is close to the doorway, and Arella has to watch the edge of her cloak for catching fire as she skirts around it. She finds Nashoba making beds at the back of the cave.

"Hey you." She says, a little shy. *"Why am I shy? I know this man."*

"Hey." He says, not really looking at her. This confuses Arella. She hates how he's being with her at the minute.

"What is wrong with you?" The unexpected anger in her voice making Nashoba look up. Arella's eyes look mad. Nashoba hasn't seen her look like this ever. It's almost like the anger has darkened her eyes. It's a little frightening. He looks behind her at the others. They don't seem to have noticed, to busy preparing the boar and laughing about something.

"What do you mean what's wrong with me? I'm making the beds." He answers, although he knows exactly what she means.

"You know exactly what I mean Nashoba." Arella is struggling to keep her voice low. She peeks behind herself, seeing that the others are paying her no attention. Only Maska and Nashoba are listening to her. "Why do you treat me different around them?"

"I...I..." Nashoba doesn't know how to answer.

"Are you ashamed of me?" Her voice breaks a little but she regains herself. He will not see her cry or break.

"No I'm not ashamed of you." Nashoba answers, a little shocked by her anger. "I just..."

"You just what?"

"I don't know what they would think if they knew about us."

"What do you mean?" This has hurt Arella. The pain in her chest wells up. *"His is ashamed of me."* She looks directly into his emerald green eyes. "Do you like me or don't you?"

"It's not that simple." Nashoba answers.

"Well you need to make your mind up." Arella folds her arms across her chest, feeling the stone wolf warm against her skin. Nashoba reaches a hand out to her, one eye on Nootau and Mato by the fire.

"Of course I like you but..."

"No." Arella pushes his hand away. "No buts Nashoba. You either like me or you don't. But you need to make your mind up. I'm not a little girl, and I'm not playing games." Arella reaches into her cloak, feeling for the red stone wolf at her chest. She tugs at the leather holding it around her neck and it comes free in her hand. She holds it out for him. "This it yours."

"Arella I gave it to you." Nashoba says.

"No Nashoba." She sighs. "I don't want it. This is yours to give to the one you want to spend your life with. And that's not me." Dropping the wolf to the floor in front of Nashoba, she turns away from him. Looking over her shoulder as she walks away. "You need to grow up Nashoba and decide what you really want in life before its too late."


Arella walks towards Nootau and Mato, followed closely behind by Maska. She looks out of the cave into the forest nearby. The sun looks to be going down, and darkness will soon fall on the land. A slight shower of snow has begun to fall. "I'm going out for a walk. Take a look around and scout up ahead." Arella says, pulling her cloak up over her head, making sure he fur is tight to her face. "I'll be back before the boar is cooked."

"Okay." Nootau and Mato chorus. Maska starts following her.

"I'm going alone Maska, if you're okay with that?" He looks at her a little confused but decides to stay back with the men anyway. Saves him getting wet fur.

There isn't much wind today, and the falling snow is beautiful. It has started settling on the cold hard ground and some of the pine trees leaves have dusting's. Arella looks around at the forest as she walks, beautiful but eerie. As she walks down the centre of the tree line, making sure she keeps track of where she has been, Arella notices something. The sound of the falling snow seems to have dulled the sounds of the forest. The creaking of the old trees is dulled, and the noises the animals make seem to have all but gone.

Arella peeks behind herself, looking back at the dim light from the cave they are calling their home tonight. She can hear the faint laughter of the men that inhabit it. This gives her comfort, knowing they are close by should she need them. Looking up at the vast mountain above her Arella strains her eyes. The white of the snow glares in the dying light of that day, shining and shimmering like something out of this world. The snow looks thicker the higher up she looks, and thin clouds seem to cover the top of the mountains, making it impossible to see the peeks. The trees seem to gradually become thinner and thinner, meaning there will soon be no wood for them to use for fire building. Arella makes a mental note to collect enough dry firewood and tinder before they reach that point.

Looking up at the mountains above Arella squints. *"I'm sure there's something up there."* She looks harder. A figure is standing on the mountain. Arella can't make out whether it is a man or woman, but there is definitely a person up there. "Guys quick!" She shouts over her shoulder, attracting the attention of the men in the cave. They all burst out of the entrance, afraid that something might be wrong.

"What? What is it?" Nashoba shouts back. He is the first to reach Arella, closely followed by the others. "What's wrong?"

"Nothing's wrong, just look up there." Arella points to the mountain where she saw the figure.

"All I see is rocks and snow." Nootau shivers. He's removed his fur cloak in the warmth of the cave, now only in bare arms, the hair standing on end. "I'm going back in, it's far too cold for me."

"It was there." Arella says. "A person I swear."

"How could there be a person up here Arella? No one lives this far up." Mato argues.

"And who would be in the mountains at this time of winter." Nashoba argues. "Except us of course."

"It was there." Arella squints harder, this time picking the figure out of the rocks again. It's moved, and is now a little closer. She is still unable to tell if it is a man or woman, but realises why the others did not see it. She was pointing them in the wrong direction. She takes hold of Nashoba's hand and points his finger towards the mountain in the right direction. "See, there." Nashoba now sees the figure, and he points it out to the others.

"Well I'll be. There is a person up there." Nootau says, still shivering.

As they watch the person on the mountain, snow falling lightly around them, the figure seems to change. It grows larger, taking a new form. None of them can quite believe their eyes. It grows larger, then goes down on all fours, taking the shape of a massive bear. Nashoba looks to Arella, a look of fear on his face she has not seen before. "Skinwalkers."

# Chapter 2

The fire has heated the cave up nicely, the walls holding the heat inside, keeping the new winter chill at bay. Arella removes her cloak as she enters the warmth, revealing her bare arms beneath. The others all follow suit, except for Nootau. He was out in the snow without his cloak, and grabs for it as soon as it is within eyesight. "Bloody hell it's freezing out there!"

"So what is a skinwalker?" Arella asks the group as she hangs her cloak on a sharp stone on the cave wall.

"You can't tell me you don't know what a skinwalker is." Mato laughs, as do the others. All with the exception of Nashoba. He isn't laughing, or smiling or even looking at her. Arella feels bad for hurting him, but he needed to know he was hurting her.

"I'm serious guys. What are skinwalkers?"

"Looks like no one ever told her about them." Nootau says. "Nashoba, you're the best at telling this story." He looks at the red wolf expectantly.

"I don't feel much like storytelling." Nashoba answers back, a little childishly. Arella notices the stone wolf in his hand. He's turning it between his fingers endlessly. "You tell it this time."

"Suit yourself." Nootau laughs. "Get comfortable, this is a good story."

Now seated together, with Nashoba sitting a little way off, Maska curled up close to Arella's side purring all the while and the smell of the cooking boar filling their nostrils, Nootau begins telling Arella about skin walkers. He is very animated as he speaks, and Arella is completely engrossed in his story. "Long ago there used to be a tribe that lived in the forests to the north. They were a large tribe with many people. They hunted the animals that lived in the forest, and gathered berries and fruit from the bushes and trees. They lived in peace with the forest for years, never killing unless they needed to, never harming the land intentionally, life was amazing." Nootau swings his arms around as he talks, exaggerating everything he says. "The people in this tribe also has friends, a bit like your Maska. They made friends with some of the animals in the forest, and each of the warriors took a companion. Some had wolves, others eagles, but the chief's companion was a big brown bear." Arella's shock is clear on her face.

"So others used to do what I've done with him?" Arella looks down at the great auron cat next to her, the purple in his black fur shining in the light of the fire.

"In a way yes." Nootau continues. "Although they were not the same as you and Maska. This tribe began to use their animals for more than just hunting. They had a way of talking to them, as if they understood each other without having to talk or communicate in anyway that anyone else would understand. They decided that they were too good for to be just warriors, they wanted more than that. They wanted to rule all of the tribes in the area. They were clearly the most powerful people in the land, so they should rule the land."

"How did they come to that conclusion?" Arella asks.

"It's simple." Nashoba interjects. Arella is shocked to hear him speak, thinking he was sulking for the night. "They thought they were better than everyone else. A gift from the gods." He shoots her a hateful look. *"So that's how he thinks I see myself."* Arella scowls at Nashoba. The others notice this, but none of them question it. They've all noticed that things between Arella and Nashoba have been testy over the last week or so, but none of them mention it. Not in front of Arella anyway.

"Anyway..." Nootau breaks the silence Arella didn't notice had filled the cave. "They all, with their animal companions, set out to the nearest tribe. The chief's bear was the one to do most of the damage. He set it on the chief and his children, tearing each of them apart, even the baby his wife has birthed just the day before. It was a massacre, bodies everywhere. Some of the women and children were spared, but not the men or the old. They slaughtered them all." Arella can't help but be shocked by this.

"But why would they think this was right?" Nootau doesn't

answer his question, only continues with the story.

"They did this with all of the tribes around them. With each tribe they slaughtered, the warriors became more like the animals they owned. The chief grew taller, the ones with wolves got faster, and the ones who owned the eagles became more ruthless." His face turned dark and Nootau took on another face as he told the next part of the story. "They started losing who they were, their personalities disappearing. They started changing the way they looked too. Some of the men grew beards, and became scruffier. It got worse the more tribes they killed."

A cold wind blows through the cave, causing Arella to shiver. Mato begins stripping meat off the cooking boar and handing it out to everyone. Nootau continues on with the story. "One day, the son of the chief was walking in the woods. He came across a pool of water. He looked at himself in the clear water and didn't like what he say. He had grown harrier and thin, the hair on his head was messy and dirty. He bared his teeth at the pool, not recognising his own face. Sharp teeth filled the mouth of the stranger staring back at him, his eyes turned yellow rather than brown. The chief's son could no longer recognise himself and went into a rage fit. He took off further into the forest, rage and anger coursing through his veins. He began to shout and scream, the shouts sounding more and more like the howl of the wolf he was becoming." Another shiver ran down Arella's spine. "His skin began ripping, and beneath the skin dark brown fur appears." Nootau stands up to emphasise his point, ever the drama queen. He raises his arms in the air. "His arms started changing as he looked at them, his hands changing into paws, claws coming free from the ends, fur covering everything. His body changes as well, and the howls became stronger. His wolf ran to his aid, hearing his cry out in pain, but was not met with a man, but another wolf." Arella can't help but gasp.

"How is that possible though?"

"No one knows, but that's the legend of the skinwalkers. From that day on, the other members of the tribe began turning into their animals. Some can turn back into their human form, while others were stuck that way." Nootau finishes.

"A load of rubbish I say still." Nashoba says, clearly still sulking.

"How can you say it's rubbish?" Mato argues. "We just saw one."

"We don't know what we saw." Nashoba spits back, a scowl on his face.

"Right." Mato shouts, causing Maska to jump. He'd fallen asleep leaning against Arella's leg. "I've had enough of you Nashoba. What is wrong with you. You've been in a mood now all night."

"Nothing. I'm fine." He lies, but no one is buying it. "Just leave me alone."

"No I won't leave you alone." Mato continues. "Something has made you in a mood and I want to know what."

"It's nothing, just leave it!" Now Nashoba is shouting too.

"Enough the both of you!" Arella brings her voice louder than the bickering men. "If Nashoba wants to wallow in his own self-pity then let him. I'm going to sleep. We have a long days treck ahead of us tomorrow."

"You're one to talk." Nashoba answers back.

"What do you mean I'm one to talk?" Arella uses her hands as quotation marks. "I don't wallow in my self-pity."

"No but you do cause others pain don't you."

"And what does that mean?" Nashoba's eyes dart to the other men in the cave. He decides better of having this argument now.

"Never mind Arella."

"No I want to know as well." Nootau buts in. Mato nods his agreement. Now Nashoba has no choice but to tell them all what has been bugging him.

"I'd rather not go into it." He tries.

"No go on Nashoba. Tell us all what's been bugging you all night." Nootau pushes. Arella is feeling pretty guilty for making him tell everyone like this, but it has to be done. He has to prove that he wants to be with her. If he doesn't then she will get over it, she'll be okay. But if her does, then he has to prove it, he has to grow a pair and speak up. *This is it. He tells them and I know we can work. If he doesn't, there might not be anything in it for us.*

"It's just…" Arella's heart beats faster. "I just…"

"Go on." They all urge.

"I'm worried there might be nothing there at the top of the mountain when we get there." He finally says, looking at the floor. His green eyes sad when he looks up at Arella. Her heart drops at the same time as her heart. It feels as though it has literally been ripped from her chest. She catches herself, pulling her mouth closed again before the others notice. Nashoba's looking directly at her, but all noise around her has gone. She simply shakes her head, the cold digging its way into her very being.

"I'm going to bed." She says, and without another word, Arella moves to the bed furthest from Nashoba. She removes her boots and climbs inside facing the wall.

The corner she has chosen is dark. Maska lays at her back, soaking up the heat from the fire. Arella is shivering, but it is not from the cold. The cave itself is pretty warm. It is her heart that is cold. She wraps her arms around herself, holding herself together so she doesn't fall apart. A silent crystal tear falls in the dark.

"I wonder what's up with Arella." Nootau whispers, although she can still hear him.

"She's just tired." Nashoba lies, knowing exactly what it is that's upset her enough to take her straight to bed. "There's far too much meat on this boar for just tonight. We'll have to eat more in the morning." He continues.

Arella closes her purple eyes. Another silent tear falls. What hurts more than him not telling the others and lying about why she is upset is the nonchalant way he moves on to talk about something else. With her back against the group, none of them will see her cry. She wouldn't want them to. They need to think she's strong, even when she isn't.

"Is she asleep?" Arella hears Nashoba say.

"I think so." Mato whispers back.

"Good." Nashoba replies. "I've been thinking and I don't know where to go from here."

"What do you mean?" Nootau asks.

"Can I tell you guys something? And you have to promise me you won't laugh."

"Tell away Nashoba. And we'll try not to laugh." Nootau quips.

"I'm not going to tell you unless you take me seriously." Nashoba sulks.

"Okay, we promise to be serious." Mato say. From the noise that follows, it sounds like Mato elbowed Nootau in the side.

"Oww. Yes we promise to be serious." He says.

"I think I like her." He says after an agonizing silence. Arella's heart does a jump for joy, then stops all together. Blood rushes to her face and she can hear her own heartbeat in her ears. *"He said he likes me."*

"Well you took your time to say it." Nootau says.

"What?" Nashoba sounds shocked. "What do you mean?"

"We all saw it." Mato laughs, his booming voice just a little too loud.

"Shh." Nashoba quietens him. "You'll wake her up."

"Well why not wake her? Tell her the good news." Nootau gushes. "She likes you just as much you know."

"She told you?" Nashoba asks.

"No but it's obvious." Mato answers. "You only have to look at the way she watches you, the way she smiles when you're near her. Mate, its clear as day. The girl likes you."

"I'm not so sure." Nashoba frowns. Arella can picture the frown on his face, scrunching up his perfect features. "She gave me this back."

"Your wolf?" Nootau and Mato say at the same time. "You gave her your mothers wolf?" Nootau continues.

"I did. Well I like her. But she gave me it back."

"Why did she do that?" Mato asks, the confusion clear in his voice.

"It's complicated." Nashoba says.

"Well we've got all night, explain." Nootau pushes.

"Guys I don't really want to go into it."

"Well tough! You've got no choice." Nootau says.

"Well she gave me it back today. She said that if I wasn't going to tell you guys that I liked her, then she wasn't interested." Nashoba sulks.

"Is that it?" Mato laughs. "Well you've told us, so now you and her can go back to normal."

"Except I'm not sure we can." Arella's heart sinks. What she said hit Nashoba hard. It backfired. "Maybe she doesn't like me as much as I like her. If she did, she'd be okay with me keeping quiet right?"

"I don't think so Nashoba. You're not thinking like a girl at all." Nootau says

"What and you're so in tune with your inner girl that you know what she's thinking?" Mato asks.

"Well, no, but I have a pretty good idea." Nootau starts. "I mean look at her." Arella can feel all six of their eyes boring into her back. "The girl has been an outsider all her life. Now we let her in, and you make her feel like she should be a secret. You have to know how that would make her feel." Nootau's got Arella completely. He knows exactly how she feels. Shame Nashoba doesn't. "Does that make sense?"

"I guess so yeah." Nashoba answers, clearly unhappy about being told.

"You need to do something to prove to her that you like her." Nootau says.

"Agreed." Mato adds.

"What am I meant to do?" Nashoba asks. "I've come all the way out to the mountains for her. What more does she need?" Arella breathes in deep. This is either going to go really well, or she is going to lose her green eyed god and the others. She moves in her furs, sitting up quickly. They all turn to look at her, surprised that she is still awake.

"I need proof Nashoba." She says finally, an angry but sad look on her face. "Not just words, not just the wolf, but proof. Telling Nootau and Mato is a start, but I want more than that." Nashoba opens his mouth to speak, but Arella stops him. "All my life I have been the outsider. I want to feel normal. I want to live a normal life. Is that too much to ask?" She pauses. "Think about it this way. Would you be keeping me secret if I had dark skin and black hair?" Nashoba's silence is telling. "No I didn't think so."

Arella stands up, leaving her furs on the floor. She pulls her boots on angrily. "Arella wait please." Nashoba says.

"Let her go Nashoba." Nootau puts a hand on his shoulder. He shrugs it off angrily.

"I'm going out." Arella says, pulling her cloak on over bare arms. She picks up an extra length of fur and wraps it around her face, hiding her nose and mouth before pulling her hood up over her head. "I'll be back. Just need some time." Arella picks up her grathon, and tucks her dagger into her boot just in case. She looks out into the snow storm outside. It looks cold. Really cold. But there's nothing keeping her in the cave. She doesn't want to be near Nashoba at the minute, and the time away from him will do her good. Arella's never really been one for company. The only company she truly enjoys is her own, and that of Maska, but as he doesn't talk, it's much easier to be with him. "You coming?" She looks back at the sleepy auron cat. He takes one look at the snow outside and decides better of going out in it. He blinks his strange eyes at her and shakes his head. Arella nods back, and with that, turns to leave the cave for the second time that night.

It's now very dark outside, and the snow is laying thick on the ground. Arella shivers slightly as she walks through the forest, snow sticking to the furs she holds tight around herself. She looks up at the flurries in the sky, now beginning to slow. She breathes in deep, the smell of the mountain air fresh and clean. She walks for a good couple of minutes in a straight line. Not up the track where they will be walking tomorrow, but away from the caves. She walks towards the edge of the mountain they've been climbing. They've not gone far up it, but already they're reaching a considerable height. Arella gets to the mountain edge and looks down. Only about a hundred meters, but it looks quite high from where she's stood.

Standing back about a meter or so from the edge, Arella breathes in again. A strong gust of wind comes from in front, pushing Arella's hood back. The hood goes down and her hair blows freely in the wind. The snow has stopped now, but the icy wind has not. Arella looks out over the land, looking back at where she came from. She can just about see where her home would be from here. The moon is peeking through the thin snow clouds, and a few stars have gathered in the sky. The light shines down on the lake below, reflecting and lighting everything around it up. It's beautiful out there. Arella misses her home. "I hope all of this will be worth it." She says aloud. "I just wish I could have a sign, something to tell me I'm doing the right thing."

"You are doing the right thing." Nashoba pipes up.

"I thought I told you I was going out on my own." Arella's mad.

"You were gone a while. I wanted to check on you." He sounds nervous.

"I can handle myself." Arella bounces back, still too angry to talk properly. She turns to look at him, her white hair blowing in the wind. When she sees his face, those watery green eyes, her anger fades. The apology is etched into his face, making him appear younger than he is.

"I'm sorry." He says quietly, looking down at the snowy ground. He shuffles his feet, making patterns in the snow. Arella can't help but think of a child when she looks at him. "Can I at least explain myself?" He asks.

"You have one chance." She answers, although her sternness is failing her. It's his eyes. She just can't stay mad at him with those eyes looking so sad. "One chance." She reiterates.

"You have to understand me too." He starts. "All my life, people have had this expectation of me. I have to be the perfect son, the perfect future chief, the perfect warrior, take the perfect bride. I've never been able to make my own choices. I'm struggling here Arella." She feels for him. He's been in a similar position to her.

"Just tell me what you want." Arella says to him. "Not what anyone else would want, but what you want."

"I want you." He says.

"Well then it's simple isn't it."

"I guess so yes." He says with a smile. As he smiles, the sky around them lights up. Blues and greens fill the air, dancing in the sky. "Beautiful." Nashoba says, although he is not looking at the sky. He walks over her, the blue and green dancing on Arella's pale face. "Please take this." He holds out the stone wolf. "I want you to take it" He moves closer. Arella turns around. For the second time, Nashoba places the wolf around Arella's neck. She turns around to look at him, those green eyes mesmerising.

"Thank you."

# Chapter 3

Morning light streams in through the care entrance, shining on Arella's face. With the cold morning air seeping into the warmth of the cave, and the light from the morning sun beaming in on Arella's face, she awakens. As she opens her eyes, Arella is aware of pressure on her waist.  She looks down, careful not to move too much, and sees a familiar arm. Her stomach dances with butterflies. Nashoba is sleeping with his arm around her. She smiles to herself. All the arguments they'd had over the last couple of days, the awkward moments when they weren't talking, the silence and suppressed anger was worth it in the end. Now everyone knows that Arella likes Nashoba, and that he likes her back.

The embers in the fire have dies out now, and all Arella can smell as she lays in the furs, Nashoba's arm around her, is the boar they caught last night. With all of the arguments, Arella didn't feel much like eating, and went to bed without having eaten much. Her stomach growls loudly as she thinks about the meat on the cooked boar. Nootau had brought it further into the cave in an attempt to stop predators from stealing it. They'd also covered the front of the cave with spare furs before they went to bed. This helped to keep them warm, but seen as though Arella can still see the half-eaten boar, it would appear it worked well at keeping bears and lyron cats away. Still yet to see a lyron cat, Arella wonders what they might look like. She's heard that they are bigger then auron cats, hard to believe when she looks at him, lying on his back, legs in the air. He looks harmless now, but Arella knows he isn't. So do the rest of the men. However, if they come across lyron or auron cats in the wild, they will not be a docile as Maska. Arella must remember this.

The stone ground beneath the furs where Arella has made her bed is making her back ache. It would be a pointless idea to lay there in pain, and she needs to be up soon if they're to get a good way up the mountain before dark tonight. She gingerly lifts Nashoba's hand from her stomach and pulls herself free from the furs, careful not to wake anyone. Maska shifts his position but does not wake. Arella stretches out her arms. *"Feels nice to be up again."* She hears bones click as she moves. *"Stone is not comfortable to sleep on."* This takes her back to the last time she was truly uncomfortable. Sleeping in the tree above Nashoba's village, watching them all go about their day. *"That was a bad night's sleep."* She looks back at the group of men all laid on the floor. Nashoba hasn't noticed she's gone, but his arm still reaching for her. Nootau is drooling slightly, his mouth hanging open, and

Mato is snoring like a bear. Come to think of it, it was most likely the snoring that kept the animals away, rather than the animal skin hanging at the door. Arella has to stifle a laugh at the sight of then. *"Without all those bad night's sleep in that tree, I wouldn't be here now with them."* She smiles, feeling grateful for what she has.

The stone swords the men brought with them lay on the ground close to the boar. *"Strange they haven't had to use them."* Arella thinks. She wonders back to their journey over the last week or so. *Come to think of it, we've really not been walking all that long. It's only been just over a week, and we're already part way up the mountain. I thought it would take much longer. Then again, we don't know how far up the mountain we actually have to go."* Arella's stomach grumbles again and she remembers what it was she got up for. Moving over to the boar still on the spit, she takers her dagger, still stored in her boot but no longer on her foot, and cuts off a piece of meat. *"Not as nice cold, but it will fill a space."* She looks to the dead fire and wonders if she should get it going again before the others wake up. "Well don't offer me any of that then." Nashoba says. Arella looks over to him, rubbing his eyes, hair a mess. "Least you could do is bring me breakfast in bed."

"You're cheeky Nashoba. Has anyone ever told you that?"

"Many people yes, but I don't believe them." He laughs, pulling himself free from the furs he slept in. It is only then that Arella realises he is topless. His dark chest looks hard as stone, clearly defined muscles shine in the morning light. He pulls a top on over his head, leaving Arella wishing he'd left himself half dressed, before walking over to her. Nashoba reaches out a strong hand to Arella's, placing his fingers around her hand, but it is not the hand he is reaching for. He takes the bloodglass dagger from her and begins slicing away at the boar. Taking a chunk for himself, and handing one to Arella too. "Sleep okay?" He says, mouth full of food. It's rather unattractive, but Arella doesn't care.

"I guess so yeah. The ground's a bit hard though." She admits.

"I thought it wasn't too bad." He says, his messy hair all over his face. He looks so young like this. "It was warm at least."

"That I'll agree with." She laughs. She takes another bite of the cold boar meat, the cooled fat rough and a little bitter on her tongue. She pulls a face as she bits into it.

"Not so nice cold is it." Nashoba says, clearly having the same experience as Arella.

"Better than nothing though." Arella reluctantly says. "We should get moving soon. Days are getting shorter, and we need to make it to the edge of the treeline before nightfall."

"How come? Wouldn't it make more sense to move slower, that way we get another day in the forest." He asks.

"If we do that, then we might reach the edge long before dark.

We'd have wasted a day completely, and left ourselves open to more predators." She explains.

"True." Nashoba replies. "But it will be cold in the mountains without the trees to shield us from the wind." He frowns. "How will we get past the cold?"

"My plan is to gather some branches for fires further up the mountain. That way we can stay warmer at night and we can cook food if we find it. But I think we might need warmer clothes too."

"Ahh, now I thought ahead on that one." Nashoba pipes up. The others are beginning to wake now, but not joining in with the conversation. "I packed extra furs because I knew it would be cold. We've been through snow before, and it wasn't nice. They're in the pack over there." Nashoba points at one of the skin bags they brought with them. They were lucky to still have all of their belongings. Especially after they came across that thing in the forest on the other side of the canyon. Arella walks over to the pack, picking it up. She wasn't allowed to carry this, so never got a feel for how heavy it was.

"This weighs a lot Nashoba." She says to him. "There must be a lot of furs in there."

"It's not just furs. I packed furry cloaks for the rest of us. I know you have yours but we're going to get cold in those." Nashoba gestures towards the cloaks he, Nootau and Mato had been wearing. They're thinner than Arella's fur one, and made only from the hide of deer. "There's also fur lining for out boots and extra furs for sleeping in. I think that's everything."

"I forgot we brought all of that." Nootau pipes up.

"Of course you did." Mato joins in. "You weren't carrying it." They all laugh.

"Glad to see you're awake." Arella says. "Fancy some cold fatty boar for breakfast?"

"Not really."

"No."

"Well it needs eating, and you need to keep your strength up. It could be the last meal we get in some time." Nashoba says. "We don't know how much food there will be higher up the mountain."

"I'll catch anything we see on the way. That way we at least have a meal tonight." Arella says. "But food will not keep long enough to keep us going through the rest of the journey."

"Won't meat keep a few days?" Nootau asks. "I mean, it's cold enough up here."

"It will last a couple of days yes, but not long enough." Arella answers. "And dead animals aren't exactly light you know."

"True. But once we're wearing the extra furs, that frees up both the skin bag and the weight that we would have been carrying." Nashoba points out.

"True." Arella says. "I didn't think of that. We might just be able to do this then." She smiles. Things are looking up, and the sky last night was further proof that she is doing the right thing. "Come on guys. We need to eat this meat." She looks to Maska. Just waking up, licking his lips at the smell of the boar filling his nostrils. "If we don't eat it, Maska will get fat." They all laugh at this, except for Maska who scowls at Arella. "I'm joking Maska. But seriously, tuck in." With this they do start eating. None of them are happy to be eating the fatty meat. Once cooled, the fat turns lumps and gritty. Not a nice texture. But it will keep them going through the cold.

Once Arella, Nashoba, Nootau and Mato have had their fill of the boar, which is not very much due to texture, Maska takes over. "Do we change into the furs now, or wait until later when it gets really cold?" Nootau asks. It's clear he feels the cold more than the others.

"I think we should wait." Arella says. "Better to be a little cold for today, then put the furs on before leaving the trees tomorrow. That way we will feel the benefit when we change into them." Everyone agrees with this, although Nootau is a little reluctant.

"Maska." Nashoba says to the great auron cat. He looks up from the boar at his big paws, the fat white on his black fur, his odd coloured eyes blinking at the dark man saying his name. "When you're finished we'll get going." Maska nods his head then continues eating.

"From the looks of it he won't be long." Arella says. She's knelt on the floor, sharpening her bloodglass dagger with a flint. Sparks fly from it as she does so.

"I swear you sharpen that thing every day." Nootau laughs.

"I have to." Arella says, not looking up from her red dagger. "If I don't keep it sharp, how will I catch your dinner?" She smiles. Maska moves next to her, licking his lips and cleaning his paws. "Ready?" She asks him. The auron cat blinks at her, then stands and walks towards the cave entrance. "I'll take that as a yes."

With all of their belongings on their backs, the group begin walking up the mountain. Still following the faint path through the mountains, they walk quickly. Frozen snow crunches beneath their feet, sparkling in the sunlight. Snow now covers the trees around, making everything white and clean. Arella can see her own breath in front of her, the water crystallising as she breathes. They walk in relative silence, none of them having to say much. This goes on for a good hour or so, before they decide to take a small break. "But we haven't been walking long." Nashoba says.

"No but we are cold. And walking through the snow is hard." Nootau complains.

"It's not just that." Arella says. "We need to make sure we're going in the right direction." She moves towards a tall tree with a thick base. She looks up to the top. "I'm going to climb up here, make sure we're heading the right way through the mountains."

"But we can see that we're going up." Mato says as Arella places one boot on a low handing branch to push herself up.

"But we can't see from here which direction the top is." She says. "If I get to the top of this tree, I can see which way we should go."

"Look for green." Nootau says.

"What do you mean 'look for green'? There won't be any. The mountains are too cold for anything to grow up there." Arella questions.

"I had a dream last night. There was snow everywhere, but then there was green. Grass, trees, flowers, all surrounded by snow." He blinks, not quite believing his own dream. "It's just a feeling Arella, but look for green."

With one sure foot in front of the other, and deft hands that pick out the cracks and crevices in the trees bark, Arella climbs with ease. She's been doing this since she was a child, and the snow isn't making it that much harder to climb. She reaches the top in no time at all, and is soon staring at the side of the great mountain they have to climb. With the sun glaring down on her, reflecting off the snow, Arella is finding it hard to see anything. "What do you see?" Nashoba shouts up from below.

"Just snow, ice and rock." She shouts back down. Looking closer at the mountain, she thinks she can see a path winding up the rock face. She squints at the path. "I think I see a path." She shouts down.

"How can there be a path?" Nootau shouts up. "No one lives…" His voice trails away.

"Just skinwalkers." Arella finishes his sentence for him. She looks more. Then her gaze moves up the mountain. *"Can it be? No the sun must be playing tricks on my eyes."* She looks again, rubbing her eyes. *"No it really is green. There is green up there on the top of the mountain. Nootau was right."* She's started to get excited now. Nootau's dream was real. With her eyes fixated on the green at the top of the mountain, Arella shouts down. "You were right Nootau. There is green at the top of the mountain." No answer, only silence from below. Something's wrong. Arella looks down, but can't see the men below, nor can she see Maska. She descends quickly, eager to find out why her friends are not answering her.

In her panic, Arella steps on a branch unable to carry her weight, causing her to slip from about half way down the tree. She reaches out a hand in an attempt to stop herself, but the branch she takes hold of also snaps. She lands hard on the frozen ground. Her head hits the ground with a crack, causing her to momentarily black out.

Icy cold burns her face. The stinging is unbearable. Arella pulls away from the snow on the ground, her face numb with the cold. Her fingers are numb too. She pulls her arms closer to her, sitting on the ground, her arms wrapped around herself, shivering. *I've never been this cold in my life."* She stands up, using the tree she fell from as leverage. Her fingers sting as the bark catches them, more tender in the cold. She looks at them, blue and purple. Arella pulls her cloak over her head. It's wet on the outside, but thankfully the inside has stayed dry. She reaches for her granton and bow. Lucky she left them on the ground when climbing. They would have broken in the fall fro sure.

A sudden pain in her right leg draws Arella's attention as she steps forwards. "Ahh." She looks down at her leg, the bottom of her trousers are wet, and not from the snow. She reaches down, pulling her dagger from her boot. It had cut her when she fell. She moves over to a rock and sits down, pulling her trouser leg up to expose the wound. The cold has stopped most of the pain, and slowed the blood-flow, but the cut is long. Not so deep, so should heal okay, but with no barrow berries, Arella is going to have to deal with the wound herself. She digs around in the pocket of her cloak, sure there is a spiny needle in there somewhere. A prink on her finger tells her she's found the spine. She looks up at the white wilderness around her, silent and dead. *"I wonder where they are."* Panic fills her again. *"It's like when I lost Maska all over again."* She knows she must leave soon, try to find them, but her leg needs fixing first.

The packs the men were carrying are still on the ground, evidence that they left, or were taken, in a rush. Arella hobbles over to one of the packs, the one with furs inside. With her body warming up again, the bleeding in her leg is getting worse. She roots around in the bag until she finds what she was looking for. Reeds from grue bulbs. Arella always kept a couple handy, knowing they're useful for sewing clothes up, or fixing the bow string on her bow. But now she has a different use for the strings within the reeds. She's going to use it to sew her own leg up.

With needle and string in hand, Arella pushes the skin together on her leg. This is painful, but what is to come next will hurt even more. She takes hold of one of the spare furs she was using as a scarf and bits down hard on it. Arella's hand is shaking and she brings the needle to her flesh. "Man up!" She mutters through the furs in her mouth. She pushes the needle through the fresh white flesh and brings it out the other side. She moans through gritted teeth, but continues to sew. *"If I don't get this sewn up, I'm either going to lose too much blood to walk, or get an infection."* She pushes through the pain and closes the wounds. Her hands now bloody, and with a sick feeling in her stomach, the wound is sewn and no longer bleeding. Arella takes in deep breathes, calming and willing herself not to be sick. She places her head between her legs in an attempt to stop the dizziness ensued by the sight of her own blood. After a few minutes of this, with her eyes closed and breathing deep, Arella is feeling better.

Leaving the lower half of her leg exposed, Arella pulls her cloak tight around herself. Although there is no wind today, and the sky is clear, it is bitterly cold. She takes her scarf and wraps it around herself, bringing it up over her mouth and nose. *"This will keep me a little warmer."* She looks around for clues of where her friends have gone, and instantly finds footprints.

Stashing the bags of furs and other belongings they were carrying with them is key. Arella knows she will not be able to carry them all with her. And if they need help when she finds them, she can't have bags to burden her. She looks around, finding a small cave hidden mostly by a dead tree. Here she hides her belongings, including her dagger. "Don't want that on me at the moment."

Armed with only her grathon, bow and arrows, Arella sets out in search of her friends.

# Chapter 4

Footprints in the snow are easy to follow. It doesn't take long for Arella to find what she hoped she would not. Voices fill the air, but not voices she was hoping to hear. The sun is setting now, and a large fire helps her in finding them. The flames roar high in the sky already. Arella lowers herself down, pulling her bow from her back in case it is needed. She knocks an arrow and stalks forwards, keeping her knees bent and her body low. She pulls the furs closer to herself, hoping to hide herself from view. The furs she is wearing are pale, but not as white as the land around her.

She moves as close to the voices as she can, while trying to stay hidden. The plentiful rocks are helping to hide Arella, but she knows she will be spotted soon enough if she stays in one place too long. She skirts around the outside of the camp, taking in everything around her. From the looks of it, there are six people here, although she can't see any of their faces. They wear animal furs, and their skulls with the fur still on sit on their heads, obscuring their faces from view. *"I don't like this. It's too much like Wolf and her disciples."*

Furs of all different types hang on trees. There are coats she recognises, boar, deer, wolf and even bear. Then there are others she does not know. One of which is large and white. Assuming this is a lyron cat's coat, Arella begins to worry more. *"If these men brought down a lyron cat, what would they do to my Maska and the men. Come to think of it, I don't remember seeing any feline footprints when following. Perhaps they picked him up, or maybe he got away."* Arella hopes it is the later, but her doubts are creeping in.

As she moves around the camp, taking in everything, Arella spots a crude looking cage. She moves towards it, and spots people inside. Her people. Nashoba, Nootau and Mato are inside the cage, along with a scrawny looking boy, perhaps only ten or eleven years old. The boy spots Arella, and seeing that she is free and unlike his captors, starts shouting. Nashoba quickly catches Arella's eye and clasps his hand over the boys mouth to quieten him. The men in the centre by the fire look over. Arella quickly hides herself again, thankful for the growing dark. One of them looks over at the cage, and Arella gets a look at his face. It is horrible, covered in scars similar to the one Mato has, but not well healed. The scar covers most of his face and is a nasty red colour. It looks wet too. Then Arella realises. This is not a scar but a fresh cut; very fresh from the look of the blood stain on his furs. This man wears wolf furs, the skull of the grey wolf resting on his head. Underneath, Arella can see no hair. The man looks to be bald. Arella's never seen anyone bald before, other than babies that is, and this man is clearly not a baby.

The man walks towards the cage, a club made from a big bone in his hand. If Arella had to guess, she would say the bone of a bear. "What's all the noise about?" He shouts at the cage. Nashoba has let go of the boys mouth. "Speak up boy!" The man booms. His voice is deep and terrifying. A drop of blood from his face falls onto the white snow below, spreading and turning it crimson.

"N...N...Nothing." The boy stammers.

"Well shut it then!" The big man booms again, hitting the side of the cage with his bone club. He storms off back towards the men by the fire.

"What was that about?" A smaller man asks. This one Arella notices has a hooked nose. He's skinny, all bone and sinew. He has an eagles head atop his, and its feathers all over his clothes. The wings decorate his back.

"Piggy's squealing again?" Another asks, this one with a bear's skin over him. His massive shoulders shake as he laughs. He scratches his head with claw like fingers.

"They won't be squealin' for long when we get 'em cookin'" Another says. This one looks similar to the one with the cut face and wolf skin. He also wears wolf, but this one is brown rather than grey.

Arella tries to drown out their talking, but the conversation is hard to not listen to. She can tell by the looks of them that they aren't normal, and has a growing fear that they might be skinwalkers. They all look very much like the furs they wear, although she hopes that this is just coincidence. Creeping towards the cage, Arella positions herself behind it, peeking through the gaps to make sure none of the skinwalkers can see her. Upon closer inspection she realises what the cage is made of. Bones, and from the look of them, some are human. She feels sick to her stomach, but presses this from her thoughts. Nashoba has shifter in the cage and is closest to her. He reaches a hand out to her, which Arella willingly takes. "Are you okay?" She whispers, peeking through the bars at the men by the fire. They aren't paying the cage any attention, only laughing between themselves.

"Well we're alive. But it's not good." Nashoba admits.

"What happened?" Arella asks. "I climbed the tree, and when I got down you were gone."

"They took us." Nashoba notices the bare skin on her leg and the wound that goes with it. "What happened to your leg?"

"It's fine. We have to get you out of here." Arella rushes. "Where's Maska?"

"He got away just in time. Ran off into the trees. Did he not come back when you got down?"

"No. He was nowhere to be seen." Arella scowls. Partly mad about him running off, but worried about why he hasn't come to find her.

"We'll find him." Nashoba squeezes her hand tight.

"First we get you out."

"How do we do that?"

"I don't know. But I'll find a way."

Letting go of Nashoba's hand is hard. He was holding on so tight. They look so scared in the cage, but Arella has to leave them. She's not going to be able to get them out from there. The bones of the cage are too thick. Some of the bones look to still have skin on them, and there is a foul smell of rotting flesh about them. The image of a rotting fox fills Arella's mind, the maggot writhing in its skull, the smell of death. A flashback from Wolf and her disciples and their camp. This place is too similar, and Arella doesn't like it. It scares her. *"What if these people are related to Wolf and her disciples? I bet they are."* She shudders at the thought.

Shouting from the fire drags Arella back into the present time. "Bring 'im 'ere." The brown wolf skinwalker calls.

"Which one Hemene?" The other with the wolf skin shouts back. Looking at them, Arella thinks they're twins. They look almost identical, except for the cut on the grey ones face.

"The skinny boy." He shouts back. "Don't think that one'll last much longer. Better have him first." A sly smile fills his face. The grey wolf man strides over to the cage.

"Enyeto will be pleased with this one." The grey wolfed man says.

"*Who's Enyeto?*" Arella thinks. Then it dawns on her. She's just realised what the men are talking about.

The boy begins screaming again. "No, no not me!" IT all happens so quickly, but seems to move in slow motion. The grey wolf man reaches out towards the cage, puling at the leather straps keeping it closed. They undo and the door falls open. The young boy cowers at the back of the cage, Nashoba guarding in front of him.

"You're not taking him!" He spits in the face of the grey wolf.

"I can take you instead if you want." Grey wolf laughs back at him.

"No." Hemene insists. "Enyeto would want t' little one. Bring 'im 'ere now."

"Yes brother." Grey wolf says. "Togquos will bring the skinny boy to the fire for Enyeto." IT becomes apparent that the grey wolf is talking about himself. He reaches into the cage again, his big arms pushing Nashoba to the side. Arella can't believe what she is watching, but there is nothing she can do about it. With the only men that could help her caged up and without weapons, and her auron cat missing, Arella would have no chance against this group of men. It pains her to watch the scene that unfolds in-front of her, but she is unable to do anything about it.

Nashoba's green eyes catch Arella's. She looks over to him, a sad expression on his face. He wants to help the boy as much as she does, but he's in no fit state to fight. Arella shakes her head at him. *"There's nothing we can do."* Nashoba bows his head in disgrace, and so do the others.

"You can't let them take me!" The boy yells, tears falling from his eyes. This brings a tear to Arella's eyes also. Everything slows down as Togquos yanks the boy from the cage. He holds onto the door for dead life, his fingers clasped around one of the bones, refusing to let go. "I don't want to die!" He cries louder.

"Shut him up Togquos!" The man with the eagle head calls over. "He's giving me a headache."

"I'm trying Kwahu, but he's stronger than he looks."

"Notaku, get o'er there 'n 'elp." Hemene says to the man with the bear skin. He stands from his seated position, his absolute size becoming apparent. He stomps over to Tagquos and the boy who's name Arella did not know.

"Can't do anything right can you?" He booms. "Here, give him to me." Natoku grabs the boys thin arm and yanks. The audible snap makes Arella cringe, and the boy scream even louder. He then goes silent, passed out from the pain. Arella opens her eyes again and looks at the boy, now hanging limp in the giant man's arms, his own arm clearly broken, bent at a funny angle, the bone jutting out of the skin.

"Is he dead?" Arella hears Mato ask.

"I don't think so, still looks like he's breathing." Nootau answers. All of them look a little pale, their dark skin has lost its pink edge, not replaces by a green hew. Arella is feeling the same way too. This is horrible to watch.

"When will Enyeto be here? I'm hungry." A small man Arella hadn't paid much attention to asks.

"Soon Shima." Says Hemene. "He will be here soon mother."

*"Mother? This woman is his mother, and I assume then that she is Tagquos' mother too. Could she be the mother of all of them? That would make sense."* Arella looks closely at this woman, her long grey hair tangles beneath the animal skin on her head. It is that of a stag, its antlers large and pointed. They look to have been sharpened. Her skin is wrinkled, and her eyes sunken. This woman must be old.

"Togquos?" She says.

"Yes mother?" He answers, confirming Arella's suspicions.

"Come here." She becomes in a sweet but raspy voice. He

practically runs over to her. Arella gets the impression he is the simple one of the brothers. When he gets to her, Shima takes the bone club he was holding in his hand and hits him hard over the head with it. It makes a loud 'thunk' noise as bone makes contact with bone.

"Ow." He says simply, rubbing his head where he was hit.

"Next time I tell you boys to do something, you do it properly." She screams at them, her once sweet voice now frightening.

"What do you mean ma?" Natoka asks, confusion on his massive face. The muscles contorting. His forehead looks way too big, and if Arella wasn't so scared, the way it looks when he frowns would make her laugh.

"What did Enyeto ask you to do before he went out this morning?" She asks.

"Get the strange white girl and her friends?" Tagquos asks

"Exactly." Shima says, her calm voice once again. "And what did you bring him?"

"Three red boys. Better than one white girl." He shines proudly. 'Thunk'. Shima hits him over the head again.

"Wrong!" She screams. "He wanted the white girl, not the red boys!"

*"What would he want with me? And who the hell is he?"* As Arella puzzles over this, she looks over at Nashoba, Nootau and Mato. *"Maybe that means they will let my friends go."* Nashoba is

clearly thinking the same thing.

"Does that mean we can go?" Shima bursts into laughter. She stands up, her back bent and painful looking. The stag's skin she wears trailing on the ground as she shuffles forwards.

"Silly boy. Such a sweet looking boy." She laughs again, breaking into a coughing fit as she does so. She spits a hunk of flem onto the ground, leaving saliva dribbling from her wrinkled mouth. "Of course you cannot go. What are we to eat if you leave us?"

"Why would you want to eat us?" Nashoba asks. Arella's been thinking the same thing. She's never heard of people eating people before. It's madness. But then again, if these people are skinwalkers, then anything is possible.

"Do you see much food up here boy?" Shima asks. She answers herself before he can say anything. "No. So what are we to eat if we don't eat you?"

"Why don't you just live further down the mountain where there is food?" He asks.

"Because there are evil things lower in the mountain. An evil creature with a stags head, long arms and a horrible body. We barely got away from it when we fled up here." She says, genuine fear in her voice.

"But why did you come up here in the first place?" Nashoba asks.

"To escape the white girl." Another voice speaks. It is semi-familiar, but why would it be. Arella has no reason to know these people. They live far from her home, and she's never been here before.

"Enyeto, you're home." Shima calls, joy in her voice. "My brave son come to me." She takes him in her arms, holding him tight. "Did you find what you were looking for?"

"Yes mother." He answers. His voice cracked and raspy. "I've found where the red bear lives. High in the mountain, where the green grows. We will have to stay away from him. I don't like him."

"Okay my sweet. We will stay away from the red bear." She kisses his cheek. "Now go on precious. Tell the red boys about why we left our homeland to come to this godforsaken mountain."

"Like I said, the white girl." The man pulls comes clearly into view now. A bison's skin and head cover him, the horns black and sharp. He pulls this head back, revealing his face below. It is scarred, with a mark on his cheek. But that is not the first thing Arella notices. It's his neck. This is scarred also, the white lines and gashes cover the flesh. It looks as though his neck has been ripped open. How could someone survive that kind of injury, and why would he know Arella. Then it dawns on her. This is Bison. Somehow he survived Maska's bite. And now he wants revenge.

Arella's heart begins to pound. A hot sick feeling rises up inside her. *"He was dead. Maska killed him. He tore his throat out. I saw the blood."* The image brings itself to the front of her mind. All that blood, and the horrible gargling noise he made. Arella looks up at Nashoba, who is looking down at her. Bison looks towards where Arella is hiding, unable to see her in the dark.

"As I was saying." Bison continues. "Me and Myla, my lovely wife, were trying to have children. Every time we'd tried, they came out twisted and deformed. They didn't live long. The more animals we killed, the healthier our children were becoming." He clears his throat. "Everything was going well, until some little bitch started stealing our kills away from us. She was killing them quicker than their intended deaths. We decided this had to stop, so we kidnapped her auron cat. We thought then that she might be like us, she might be a skinwalker. To control an animal like that, she must have been powerful. But she wasn't. She was weak. She followed us and we captured her too. We were just going to kill the cat, but the spirits presented us with her too. She would make a worthy sacrifice for the life of our child.

"She escaped us, taking the cat with her, but not before Myla scratched her, poisoning her. She was to be our last sacrifice. We would follow her until she was dead, then eat her heart. When we found her though, she wasn't dead. Instead she..." Bison clears his throat again, struggling to speak.

"She set a pack of wolves on my sons and Myla." Shima finished. "Leaving him bloody and scarred. Left for dead. It was only by chance we came across him again. We moved up into the mountains then, away from the evil white girl." Nashoba, Nootau and Mato are all lost for words. It doesn't make sense. It seems like madness to travel all the way up the mountain, simply to get away from a girl who tried to kill you, because you tried to kill her. They just stare blankly at Bison and the others.

"No I don't want to die!" The boy has woken up. Arella moves her gaze to him. He looks down at his broken arm and screams out again. "Would one of you shut him up please!" Shims calls. Although it is a demand not a request. 'Thunk'. This time the unnamed boy gets a whack on the head. It knocks him out, leaving a bloody mark on his head. Arella hopes he is dead, for what they are about to do to him is worse than death itself.

# Chapter 5

The smell of cooking human flesh that night is strong in the air. Arella hid while they killed they boy. Evidently the blow to the head did not finish him off. They instead cut off his head, leaving it to their wolves. Their wolves had been sent off in search of food just the day before they'd spotted Arella and the group on the mountains. "They'll be hungry when they get back." Tagquos says. "We'll heave them their heads." A disgusting thought in Arella's eyes. She couldn't think of anything worse than a wolf munching on her brain.

"You prize those wolves far too much Tagquos!" Natoka says. "Any man worth his weight doesn't need wolves to fight for him. He can do it himself."

"Hush Natoka. Let Tagquos feed the wolves the heads if he wants to. There's no harm in it." Shima replies.

"See, even Ma likes my wolves." Tagquos boasts.

"They're not your wolves brother, they're mine." Enyeto sniggers. "The pack belongs to me, and they will do what I tell them.

Just because you feed them, doesn't make them yours."

"But they are mine. I like them best." Tagquos argues, fat from the boys flesh dripping from his mouth.

"Enough!" Shima shouts. "I will not have boys of mine fighting over the dinner table."

"Yes Ma." They all chorus. After a few minutes of awkward silence, their conversation continues.


Arella's moved closer to the cage now. Having had a good look at the rest of the camp, she and the others must figure out how to get them free.

"We wait until they fall asleep. Then we get you out." Arella whispers to Nashoba. The skinwalkers are far too busy eating to pay any attention to their prisoners in the bone cage. The sounds of chewing and bone grinding will stay with Arella forever.


Leaning with her back against the cage, Arella closes her eyes, hoping to drown out the sounds of eating. Nashoba is sat with his back against hers, keeping her warm in the winter night, and shielding her from view of the skinwalkers.

"Why did you not get the white girl?" Bison asks.

"We couldn't see her Enyeto." Tagquos answers.

"She was up a tree." Natoka says. "And I can't climb trees.

"No but the bear can." Enyato says. "We have these gifts for a reason. We should be using them."

"So why didn't you use your ability to turn into a bison against the white girl?" Hemene asks? Arella's been wondering the same thing.

"You know I got this later than the rest of you. If I was able to do it then, Myla would still be alive."

"And your other brothers." Shima says. "Don't forget about them."

"I might have let them die anyway." Bison yawns.

"I think it's time for my boys to go to sleep." Shima says.

"Read us a bedtime story ma." Natoka smiles.

"Of course my precious."

Arella looks round from where she is hiding. Curious to see this. All six of the men, all fully grown adults are laying down on the ground to head a bedtime story. Just as though they were all children. "*Wow.*"

"Which story do you want to hear tonight?" She asks in a tender voice.

"The white skinwakler... Tell the white skinwalker story Ma." Natoka urges.

"There was once a young skinwalker called Skah. His spirit animal was a great white lyron cat. He could transform into this cat with ease, no pain, and he would not be defeated. He was due to be the next leader of his tribe. Once his father passed, he would take charge. The lyron form he took was proof of this, for only someone who is brave, strong and bound for leadership can take the form of a beast like that. One day, Skah came across a herd of bison. He decided bison would make a good meal for his family, and so transformed into the great white lyron cat. Once he'd killed the bison, he struggled to turn back into his human form.

When he got back to his tribe, they did not recognise him. They chased him off, leaving him to be alone. He was beaten with sticks, had rocks thrown at him, was screamed and shouted at. His own wife and child did not recognise him. They were afraid of him, afraid of the lyron cat, and he was scared. He didn't know how to take his human form again. He'd never changed on his own, and always had help changing back. It is unwise to change into your animal form when you do not know how to change back. But Skah was too cocky, too confident, and too stupid to remember this.

He managed to change back, but when he did, he found that his fingernails were longer and shaper. He was upset by his appearance, and in his distress turned back into the white lyron cat. He battled with the transformations for weeks, struggling to stay one form or another for long. With each transformation, it became more painful to and much harder turn back into a human."

Arella can't help but think that this story is a bad one, not a bedtime story. She wonders if this story could be true. Skinwalkers are clearly real. She's seen them, but could this story be true. Her mind begins to wander. How does someone become a skinwalker? Are they born that way? Or do they inherit the gift in another way? She reminds herself to ask Nashoba when she helps him escape.

"He was able to transform back into human form again and found himself by a lake. Skah looked at himself in the water, not recognising the man who looked back at him." Arella can see the similarities in this story to the one Nashoba told of the skinwalking wolf.

*"Maybe the story is true. I've heard it from more than one person now. Although this story is a little different."*

" His face wad twisted and changed. Longer, sharper teeth replaced the ones he once had. His eyes had changed too. They were no longer a deep warm brown, but now an angry yellow. The looked like the eyes of a cat. Hi had sprouted hair on the backs of his hands, and his face has whiskers. The can cried out in terror. He'd changed beyond belief, cursed by his skinwalker gift and the ignorance that came with it. He was becoming shorter tempered, angrier. He got a taste for raw flesh."

"What happened next ma?" Natoka asks, a childlike look on his muscular face.

"Your Grandfather happened next." Shima said. "Skah had been raiding villages, killing livestock and being a general nuisance for the tribe he used to belong to. Your Grandfather found the young skinwalker hiding away in a cave, surrounded by the bones of the animals he'd killed and fought him. The battle lasted days, and both were tired by the end. In the end your father prevailed. Killing Skah with his spear. He was scarred and bloody by the end, but Skah was dead. He was a great warrior, and his sons were great warriors after him. You will all be great warriors too my sons. Now sleep tonight. We have a big day ahead of us tomorrow."

"Is that why you don't let us change on our own?" Natoka asks.

"Yes my son. That is exactly why. Now sleep." Shima answers.

All of the men in their animal skins fell asleep quickly, their mother doing so too. A chorus of snoring erupted, and the noise was almost deafening. With the light of the fire burning dimmer, Arella begins to hatch a plan with Nashoba. Once she is sure the men are asleep, she begins talking a hushed voice. "So how do we get you out of here then?" She asks.

"The door at the front of the cage was damaged I think when they took the boy. We might be able to force it open." Nashoba suggests.

"Wouldn't that make noise?" Mato asks.

"It might." Arella sighs. "We need to think of something, but I don't know how to get you out quietly." She looks around the dimly lit camp, shivering in the cold. "I don't think I could fight them all on my own if they woke up."

"What about your bow?" Nootau asks. "Could you take them out with that?"

"I could take out a couple, but the arrows wouldn't kill them fast enough to keep quiet. Not guaranteed anyhow. We need to think of a way to get you out without making noise." She peeks over at the sleeping men, all deep in their dreamlands. They are covered with various furs of the animals they killed, as well as the skins they wear as skinwalkers. Arella can't help but think how amazing it would be to see someone turn from human into an animal. Oh how she'd love to see that. But she must not get sidetracked. Her friends lives are at risk, and she must do something to save them. Anything. She can't go onto the mountain spirit without them, and she wouldn't leave them behind now. It would be easier to go on without them. To go to the mountains alone. She wouldn't have to worry about keeping them safe, or feeding so many people. But they are her family now. And Arella does not leave family behind.

Arella's mind wanders to Maska. *"Where is he? He'll be lonely on his own in the mountains. He could be hurt. He might need me."* It's becoming too much for her. She's starting to panic again. *"I need to take my mind off Maska. He'll be okay, and when I get them out, I'll go looking for him."* She stands from her kneeling position on the ground, the wound on her leg pulling tight. A bead of blood escapes her sewing.

"Your leg looks really bad Arella. Maybe I should take a look at it." Nootau says.

"It's fine, really. We don't have time to be worrying about a little cut."

"Arella it doesn't look fine." Nashoba argues.

"Let me look at it." Nootau insists.

"Fine." She gives in, sitting back down on the ground with her leg against the cage. She pulls the leg of her trousers up, which had fallen down slightly, revealing the wounded skin beneath.

"How did you do this?" Nootau asks as he examines it.

"I feel from the tree." Arella winces as Nootau touches the tender pink skin around the wound. "My dagger cut my leg as I fell."

"It's not infected, so should heal okay, but you have to be careful on it." Nootau warns. "If you open the wound again I'm not going to be able to sew it up from in here, and you'll lose blood too quickly to do it yourself." He pauses, looking at the cut again. "Your stitches aren't bad. How did you manage to do them without passing out or losing too much blood anyway?"

"My leg was pretty much frozen. It was numb and not bleeding much." She winces again as Nootau examines it. "Hurts like hell now though.

"I'll bet."

"Anyway. We have to get you out of here. We can finish admiring my amazing stitching when we're safe. I'm going to look at the door from the outside. See how we might be able to open it." Arella moves around to the front of the cage, followed by the men inside it. One of the hinges is broken, but the other is still intact. She looks at the other side, where the bindings are that keep it closed. A large sharp bone sticks through, keeping the bars firmly closed to the door. *"If I open this, the door might fall off, and that would make noise."*

In the darkness of the night, Arella asked about the boy who was in the cage with them. Nootau explained as best he could. The boy had told them little about himself, and they weren't in the cage with him long before he was taken. But he said that he was from a tribe close by, and that his sister had been with him when they took him. He told her how the boy cried thinking of his sister, and how the men did things to the girl other than just kill and eat her. This sickened Arella to her core. *"Poor girl. What would they do to me if I got caught..."* This thought quickly leaves Arella's mind. Not wanting to linger there too long.

She peeks over her shoulder again, a sudden idea hitting her. "I think I have a plan." She smiles.

"Really?" The men chorus.

"Yes." Arella proceeds to tell the men her plan. "So you know what to do?"

"Yes." They all agree.

"Good."

"But what if it goes wrong?" Nashoba asks, obvious caution in his voice.

"It can't go wrong." Arella says. "But we have to wait until the sun is on its way up." She finishes with.

# Chapter 6

The sun is just peeking off the horizon. The men will soon be awake. Nashoba and the others have been asleep for the last couple of hours, but Arella would not allow herself to drop off. If she did, she might have missed the crucial point for escape. A wolf's howl in the distance tells her she doesn't have much time to get her friends out. It could be the pack returning, and Arella doesn't want to have to deal with them too. She stands from the snowy ground, ignoring the pain in her leg. This wakes the others, but they make no sound. Arella must be quick, and silent as the white ghost she is.

With silent footsteps, Arella moves around the outside of the camp, remembering to keep low in case one of the men wakes up. She migrates to the area where the skins of dead animals are hung. There are animals of all types here, but Arella is only after one. The white lyron coat. She pulls it down from where it hangs, a musty dead smell resonates from it. As she pulls it down, she notices the fur is not just white. There are specks of gold through the fur, and patterns. Swirls and spots cover the pelt, in different shades of white and gold. If is beautiful. She stops briefly to admire the other pelts too. They are just as exquisite. The furs have been expertly cut from their owners, and however sad it is that the animals had to lose their lives for these pelts to have been taken, Arella can't see them go to waste. There are three nice looking pelts here other than the white lyron, including tow lovely wolves, one in dark grey and the other is black, and there is also a large bear skin in a dark brown. She gathers them all up in her arms and takes them back towards the way she came from. She intends to leave them here, then they will collect them when they leave the camp. Technically this is stealing, but Arella can see that they do not need them.

Once they are on the ground, Arella pulls the lyron coat up over her head with the skull over her own. It feels strange wearing the skin like this, with paws, head and tail still attached, but it must be done for what she has planned. She has to admit though, it is rather warm. She looks up at the cage her friends are captive in and summons all her bravery.

She strides in front of the cage and stands as tall as she is able. Arella is not a small girl, but she is by no means tall either. A voice from behind her sounds. "Skinwalkers!" It says. A deep booming voice louder than thunder itself. "I command you to wake." The voice is not Arella, but rather Mato masking his own voice in place of the lyron cat. The men sleeping on the ground wake with a start at the strange voice talking to them. Natoka is the first to spot Arella in her costume.

"It's Skah!" He shouts in surprise. "Why are you here Skah?" The others are clearly too tired and confused to think.

"I, Skah, the great lyron skinwalker." Mato pauses for effect while he attempts to think of his next line. "Have come to punish you."

"Punish us?" Natoka asks, worry on his face.

"Yes punish you." Mato bellows. "You have been bad skinwalkers, terrible in fact. I am here to punish you for the terrible things you have done." The men are now all of their feet, although not all of them look like they believe the story as much as simple Natoka. "You have taken advantage of your gifts, and used them to capture and kill innocent people."

"What do you mean 'used our gifts'? I haven't used my skinwalking to kill anyone." Kwahu pipes up. "Not for a while anyway." He sniggers.

"You all have special abilities other than your skinwalking. Strength, power, cunning. These gifts have been used wrongly." Mato bellows. Arella is getting nervous now. The men have started walking closer.

"What is this?" Shima spits. "Some kind of sorcery?"

"HOW DARE YOU ACCUSE ME OF SORCERY!" Mato shouts, trying to be intimidating. "I am Skah, the great lyron skinwalker and I am here to punish you. If you do not let these men in the cage go, I will be forced to kill you all."

"An empty threat." Enyeto laughs back. "One skinwalker against all of us. I hardly think you would win." He laughs again, choking. He steps forwards, a menacing look on his face. "Tagquos, Hemene, deal with this." He commands. The twins step forwards, their clubs in hand. Arella, in the lyron skin, stands her ground as they come for her. Wolves howling becomes louder. They're almost here. Her heart beats faster with every step the men take. They come close to her, and just as they do, the wolves appear in the camp. "Good. Tagquos, your wolves have come to join the feast."

"They'll have to wait in line." Tagquos says.

"Should we let' wolves 'ave 'im?" Hemene asks, his left eyebrow lifted higher.

"I want to be the one to kill him." Enyeto says.

"*Good.*" Arella thinks. "*Just what I wanted.*" The bison Enyeto steps forwards.

"I want to tear his throat out just like my grandfather."

"Our grandfather killed Skah with a spear..." Tagquos starts. Enyeto hits him over the head as he walks past, pushing him out of the way.

"Oh shut up fool." He spits. "It doesn't matter how he dies, as long as he does." Enyeto strides straight up to Arella, or Skah, whichever. Arella takes a small step backwards, coming in contact with the cage. She taps it gently. A signal.

With the three wolves behind him, snarling and growling, Enyeto steps up to Arella. "You're smaller than I thought you would be." He laughs. He grabs hold of the furs at the front, and lifts her into the air. "Lighter too." He pulls his clubbed arm back ready to swing at her. Arella brings her arms up and pulls the head of the skin back, revealing her face. "You!" He yells, dropping Arella on the ground in shock.

"Yes, me!" Arella smiles. "Glad to see me?"

"Kill her!" He screams at the wolves, but they do not listen to him. They simply stand growling at Arella. "I said kill her!" He yells again. "Tagquos, tell your wolves to kill that bitch!"

"Is that the white girl who killed Myla?" He asks. Enyeto doesn't need to answer. The stare he gives back is answer enough. Tagquos commands his wolves to attack. They charge for Arella, snarling and growling. She steps back, fearful that they will kill her.

"Looks like the tables have turned white girl." Enyeto laughs in his raspy voice. "You will die just the way my Myla did, at the wolves jaws."

"We should bide our time my son." Shima smiles, although Arella does not like the way the smile twists on her wrinkled face.

"Put her in the cage with the others. We will kill her last."

"Good idea Ma. She can watch her friends die first, then I will let the wolves tear her apart." Enyeto laughs, once again choking. "Hemene, open that cage. If she wants to be with her friends so much, we shouldn't keep her from them." Arella looks behind herself, at the bone cage holding her friends. They look worried.

The wolves in front are still growling, but something else has caught Arella's eye. There is a black shape moving over by the far side of the camp. Arella focuses her eyed on the blackness as it shifts, staying low and well hidden. It looks up at her. One green eye, and one yellow. Maska. Her heart leaps for joy, and she quickly looks away from him. If she stares too long they might spot him. He needs to stay hidden for this to work. Arella's plan had not included him, but then she had also not banked on the wolves coming back either.

Hemene opens the cage door behind Arella and shoves her inside. She falls back in slow motion, the furs she wears cushioning the blow. The men inside the cage use the open door to their advantage, charging forwards and out of the door. Once they are out, chaos ensues. Mato has taken one of the bones from inside the cage and wields it like a club. He swings it in the air, catching Hemene on the side of the head as he leaves the open door. The wolf furred skinwalker falls to the ground, dazed and confused. His brother charges to his rescue, but Nootau takes him out. He'd taken hold of Arella's grathon. She'd left it by the back of the cage, along with her bow and quiver for them to use as weapons. Nootau trips Tagquos up with the staff of the grathon, catching the back of his leg with the bloodglass spear on the end. Nashoba heads straight for Enyeto, clear intent to kill in his eyes. He is furious that someone tried to hurt Arella. After hearing the stories, and knowing it was this man who tried to kill her, he wants nothing more than to end Enyeto's life.

Natoka stops him in his tracks, taking Nashoba by the throat. He lifts him into the air, the muscles on his massive arms showing veins as he strains to life Nashoba. "He's heavier than he looks this one." Natoka squeezes hard on Nashoba's throat. Arella can see him struggling for breath. She looks behind herself and deeper into the cage. Her bow is sitting just the other side of the bars. She stumbles to her feet and takes a step towards the bow only to be pulled to the ground again. She turns to find pressure and a hand clasped tight around the ankle of her damaged leg. She cries out in pain as he digs his sharp nails into her tender flesh. She kicks at his face with her other leg. Her foot makes contact, causing Hemene to let go. "Bitch!" He shouts, holding his now bloody and broken nose.

Reaching forwards, Arella's hands make contact with the bow.

She angles it carefully then pulls it through the bars of the cage, the quiver too. She rolls onto her back, knocking an arrow as quickly as her arms will let her. She looses it, hitting the target square. The bloodglass arrow embeds itself in the back of Natoka's bug hand, causing him to drop Nashoba to the ground like a ragdoll. He falls to the floor, gasping for air, but he's okay. "White girl hurt Natoka." He says in his strange simple way. His bottom lip has started to tremble. "Now Natoka is mad!" His trembling lip changes. He becomes angry. The ground shakes as he charges towards Arella, his face screwed up and shouting. Mato intercepts him before he gets to the cage, matching him strength for strength. They hit out at each other, punches making contact on both parts.

Hemene looks up at Arella through streaming eyes and a bloody nose. "You broke m' nose bitch!" He spits at her. He claws at her leg again, but this time she has a little help. Hemene begins shouting and screaming. "Somethin's got me leg!" He shouts. "Get it off!" Arella looks behind Hemene and spots a big black auron cat holding tight to his leg, blood seeping from the puncture holes his teeth are creating. One yellow and one green eye look up at her as he rips at the leg, pulling Arella's attacker away from her.

"Maska!" She shouts. "Boy am I glad to see you." She turns her attention to the fighting again. From the looks of it, Shima and Takoda have vanished. Running away from the fight. This is a plus for

Arella and the men, however they still have the wolves on their side. Tagquos gets up from his position on the ground. Mato had knocked his clear out, but he is coming around now. He looks wobbly as he stands, but quickly regains himself when he realises the prisoners have escaped. Tagquos calls on his wolves to attack. The first wolf lunges at Mato, knocking him over and biting down hard on his arm. It punctures flesh and Mato cries out, but the furs on his arm take the majority of the bite.

The second wolf runs straight for Nashoba, laid on the ground still catching his breath. Maska intercepts this one, diving into it before it can get a hold of him. They tumble to the floor, all teeth and claws. It breaks free from Maska and charges again for Nashoba, this time making contact. It bites his shoulder, sinking its teeth in deep. Nashoba cries out in pain. The fangs of the black wolf have gone deep into his flesh, and red beads trickle from the wound. Maska takes hold of the wolf again and pulls it back, but the damage is done

"No!" Arella screams. The wolf in front of her, the third wolf coming to kill her stops dead in its tracks. Arella stands from where she is in the cage, pulling herself from it. Hemene lays bleeding on the ground in front of her, his leg badly torn up, his face bleeding, but he's alive. Arella steps over him, and the wolf in front of her steps backwards. The other wolves in the pack also stop what they're doing.

"What?" Enyeto shouts. "Tagquos, command your wolves to kill her now!"

"Kill my puppies!" Tagquos shouts at his pack. They ignore him, snarling still, but they do not move.

"I have had enough of the killing!" Arella shouts. "I never wanted any of this." Her eyes dart down to Nashoba on the ground. He's in bad shape, and she must get him out of there quickly. His wounds need seeing to.

"If you didn't want killing, why did you kill my Myla?" Enyeto asks. The fighting has all stopped. The men stare at each other, not knowing what to do. Arella and Enyeto are staring intently at each other. Maska steps up to stand next to the white girl.

"Why did I kill her?" Arella laughs, hysteria taking over. "Why did she try to kill me? Or the other animals she murdered? Enough is enough. You either let us go, or I will have you all killed by your own wolves."

"The wolves do not belong to you!" Tagquos shouts, clearly angry at Arella for claiming them for her own. "They do not listen to anyone but me." One of the wolves growls low and deep at Arella. He's clearly the alpha of the pack. These wolves are different from the ones she is used to. Respecting them will not make them listen. Instead she tries a different tact. She stares the alpha in the eye, refusing to break stare. The wolf growls deeper, bearing its teeth.

"See, the do not like you." Enyeto laughs. "You cannot control these beasts like you did the others."

"Sit!" Arella commands. All three wolves sit on instinct, and so does Tagquos.

"Stand you buffoon!" Enyato shouts. If it weren't for the fact that their lives were in danger, Arella might have found this funny. Out of the corner of her eye, Arella spots a small smile on Nootau's face. He found it funny. "How did you do that?"

"Does it matter how I did it?" Arella answers. "All you need to know is that if you insist on killing us, I will set your own wolves on you, and you will die."

"Have it your way, white girl." Enyeto says. "You and your 'friends' may leave." Arella visibly relaxes. She looks to Mato, who instantly moves over to Nashoba to help him up. He winces in pain but once he is on his feet, manages to move of his own accord. He joins Nootau with Mato close to the back of the camp, where the furs Arella had gathered from the skinwalkers are. They pick them up.

"Maska." Arella says to the auron cat. He looks up at her then nods. He turns to walk away, and Arella turns with him. As she turns, something shiny catches Arella's eye. She turns just in time, her instincts taking over. She pulls her bow tight, knocking an arrow and firing, just as a sharp stone spear passes by the side of her face cutting it lightly. Her Arrow hits its mark, Ejyeto's chest. The man with the bison skull drops to his knees, the spear sticking out of his breast. "Come back from that you bastard." Arella says as she turns around.

The spear is sticking out of something when she turns. It has gone straight for her friends. Arella's heart sinks. "Nashoba!" She shouts, running over to him. He is on the ground, with the spear on top of him, sticking into the furs he is wearing. "No, no, no." She drops to her knees when she gets to him, fearing the worst. She moves the covers away from his face, tears falling from her own. He's pale and sweating. Tears fall faster from Arella's purple eyes. "Don't you dare die on me!" She shouts at him. "You hear me Nashoba? You cannot leave me now!"

"Arella we have to move." Nootau says. "There's a storm coming." Arella looks up at the sky. Even through teary eyes she can see the storm clouds closing in.

"We're taking him with us." She insists.

"Mato, help me with him." Nootau says. They pick Nashoba up, and the furs he is wearing come loose. A boars skin holds fast against his shoulder, the head of the spear still visible. It hasn't buried itself deep, but the wound is still life threatening.

"I'll kill you white girl." Hemene shouts after her. His brother now dead, only the two others remaining. His mother and weakest brother run off. With anger hot in her heart Arella rounds on him. She looks at the three wolves on the ground.

"Attack." She says to them. The wolves do her bidding, turning on the remaining brothers. Once again, Arella turns around and leaves behind the sound of men being ripped apart by the fangs of a wolf.

# Chapter 7

Arella bends to pick up the furs on the ground before leaving the wolves to their meal. She slings her bow up onto her back and quickly catches up with Mato and Nootau. They're walking Nashoba down the track. He's dragging his feet a little, but at least he's moving and conscious. The snow has started to fall, light at the moment, but the dark clouds above tell a different story. "We have to move him fast." Arella says, determined to get him to a cave before the storm hits.

"I don't know if we'll make it." Nootau admits. "The storm's closing in and we don't have any of our belongings."

"Don't you dare Nootau!" Arella shouts. "We will get him to a cave, and he will be okay." Nootau doesn't look too sure, and Arella cannot see Mato's face. "I will not let him die." A tear forms in her eye again. Arella urges it not to fall, but does so anyway. She wipes her face before the others can see. "Maska, could you lead the way back to where I left our things? You should be able to follow the scent." The auron cat moves to the front of the group, looking up at Nashoba as he walks past. His eyes looks sad.

Nashoba grunts, the spear clearly painful. It bounces a little as they walk, moving in the wound on his chest. Arella rushes forwards, taking hold of the spear to hold it steady. "We can't let this move about too much." She says.

"I wouldn't take it out." Nootau says. "Not until I can have a good look. We don't know what damage has been done."

"Agreed." Arella says. She looks up at Mato's face. He too looks worried. "He's going to be okay." She urges. She looks at Nashoba's face. He opens his bright green eyes, now duller than before and moans. "I promise you'll be okay." Her voice cracks on the last word and she has to turn away from him.


Arella picks up her pace and comes up on Maska. She spots a cave to the side of her and goes to investigate. When she gets to it, she finds it's not very big, but it will shelter them from the snowstorm. "In here!" She shouts. Mato and Nootau guide Nashoba over to the cave, taking him inside and out of the falling snow. Arella quickly lays out some of the furs she'd carries back from the skinwalkers camp. Nootau and Mato place Nashoba on the ground carefully, but this does not stop him calling out in pain. It hurts Arella to see him this way, and she doesn't want to leave him, but she has to go back to collect the rest of their furs and weapons. She kneels beside him and wipes sweat from Nashoba's forehead. "I promise I won't be gone long." She says to him.

"Don't do." He pleads.

"I'm sorry." Arella says. "I won't be long." She stands, pulling her hand free from Nashoba's weakening grip. She turns to Nootau. "Keep him alive."

"You can't go out in the storm." Mato says just as Arella reaches the entrance to the cave.

"I have to." Arella answers. "We need the furs, the weapons and food. If we're going to wait the storm out here and get him better, we need those things." She takes another step then pauses. "Collect as many branches as you can find, and keep warm."

With the lyron furs still on Arella's back, she sets out into the blizzard in search of the bags and something to eat. Maska has stayed behind with the men. He will protect them, and keep them warm. Arella follows the way she came from, knowing it is now not far until she gets to the place where she stashed the bags. She slips a little on the fresh snow, but the stone underneath catches her. Once she's got her footing again, she moves quicker. She does not know whether Nashoba will be alive or not when she returns. The very thought sickens her. Just when things were going so well. Now this has to happen. A pain in Arella's chest stops her in her tracks. It fills her with cold and her blood turns to ice. "Arghhhh!" She shouts out, dropping to her knees on the hard snowy ground. Flurries of the shite stuff cloud into the air, dispersed by Arella dropping so suddenly. Crystal tears fall from her beautiful purple eyes. "Why?" She asks the sky, staring up at the falling snow. Anger now replaces the sadness and Arella's face changes. The tears are still there, but the cold has gone. Her blood begins to boil and she begins shouting at the sky again. "You will not take him from me!" She shouts. "I won't allow you to take someone else I care about!" She stands up, still looking at the sky. "Everyone I have ever loved. Everyone I have ever cared about has been taken from me, and it stops now!" She marches on in determination and comes to the place where the bags were stashed. They are still there.

Arella is now looking around for prey, although she fears her caterwauling might have scared off all the game in the area. She's wrong. Arella spots something white moving on the ground. Then another one. "Mountain hares." She says to herself, a sly smile filling her lips. She knows she can catch these, and catch them easily.

Arella is distracted. She knocks an arrow from her quiver, taking aim and fires on a hare. She misses completely, embedding the bloodglass head deep in the snow. "Damn." She says under her breath. "Focus." She knocks another arrow and aims, pulling back. She breathes in deep, steadying herself, then fires. This time the arrow hits its mark, the hare's skull. It dies silently, the others have no idea what has happened. Arella takes out another hare, then another. She knocks her arrow to take out a fourth then pauses. The rabbit looks directly at her, his big black eyes focused on the arrow. Arella breathes in deep again, then pulls back and fires quick. The hare again dies silently, the arrow hitting between its eyes.

After gathering up the hares, Arella swings them over her shoulder. She walks back through the snow towards the cave she cached the furs and weapons in. They have been covered in snow, but are protected inside the bags. She puts the dead hares inside the bags as well, keeping them safe from the elements. Arella looks out over the wilderness and sighs. *"It's so beautiful up here. But so full of death."* Her mind wanders back to Nashoba as she walks back towards the small cave her friends are hiding in. *"Will he still be alive? He'd better be alive. If he's dead, I'm going to bring him back to life and kill him myself."* Another tear forms in her eye. She wipes it away with her sleeve, the fur catching the crystalline tear-drop. She looks at it, then lets it fall to the floor.

As she rounds the corner towards the cave, Arella is aware of smoke rising from the entrance. *"They got a fire going at least."* She thinks, now suddenly aware of how cold she had gotten. She shivers violently and stops. She's within eyesight of the cave, but cannot step inside. A face appears through the blizzard, then exits the cave, walking towards Arella.

"Aren't you coming inside?" Nootau asks.

"I can't." Arella answers, more tears forming in her eyes. Nootau looks at her.

"Come on Arella, you'll catch your death out here." She becomes aware at this point that Nootau is not wearing his furs. He is in only his thin shirt and trousers, boots still on his feet. She then notices the blood and the tears begin to fall.

"He's dead isn't he?" She cannot control the tears, letting them fall at will. "Please tell me he's not dead." Her heart becomes cold, and the world begins to spin. Nashoba is her world, her everything.

"Arella just come inside please." He says again. He walks towards Arella, taking her hand. "Please come inside." She pushes him away.

"I can't." She sobs. "Not if he's dead." She drops the bags to the ground, suddenly aware of their immense weight on her fragile body. She's never felt as fragile and weak as this. *"Is this what love does to you?"*

"Arella he's not dead." Nootau finally says. Her heart lifts, then fills with anger. She lashes out, hitting Nootau as hard as she can across the arm.

"Why didn't you say so in the first place?!" She shouts at him, then pushes past and rushes towards the cave.

"I was trying to tell you." Nootau shouts after her. She ignores him completely, diving into the cave as fast as her legs will carry her. When she enters, she finds Nashoba laid on the ground, surrounded and covered in furs. She goes to him straight away, kneeling beside him on the stony ground. "Nashoba. Are you okay?"

"I have a spear in my chest, but yeah I'm great." He laughs. Arella examines the wound, the spear still sticking out of his chest, but now shorter and closer to the skin.

"Could you not take it out?" She asks Nootau. He's just entered the cave, carrying all the heavy bags, dropping them to the floor as he comes through the entrance.

"I don't know what damage it's done beneath the surface." He pants, out of breath.

"We need to get him back to the village then, so someone can take a look at him, get the spear out." She rushes.

"Arella I'm okay." Nashoba insists. "It doesn't hurt all that much now. Besides, we need to keep going. We need to get to the mountain."

"We can't. Not with you like this." She panics. They've come so far to turn back now, but it might be dangerous, and she doesn't want to risk his life.

"Arella stop." Nashoba says. He takes her face in his strong hand and pulls it towards himself, kissing her square on the lips in front of the others. He pulls away after a second. "Stop worrying about me. I'm fine." Arella just smiles at him, her heart feeling warm and gooey. "I just need to rest for the night, then we'll be good to go in the morning."

"Sorry to burst your bubble..." Nootau jumps in. "But we can't go anywhere in this storm." The wind outside has really picked up, brining strong snow down on the mountainside. Whistling wind blows through the thin trees, threatening to pull them down. The cave is providing well needed shelter for now. Arella hopes the wind direction does now change. If it does, they could end up buried by the morning.

The fire burns near the centre of the cave, and the group sit around it, leaning on the three walls of the cave. I say three walls, but the cave is rounded, so more like one wall. The entrance is exposed and the wind whistles through. Arella stands, taking one of the new furs they collected, the lyron fur, and places it against the entrance of the cave. This stops the wind from blowing in, but will not stay up by itself, and Arella is not tall enough to hook it over the rocks at the top. Mato stands and walks behind Arella. "Could you give me a hand?" She asks him, expecting him to take the furs and place them himself. Instead he picks her up, as light as if she were but a child. She is now several feet taller than she used to be, and in the perfect position to place the furs. She picks up a couple of heavy rocks resting on the ledge above the entrance, and places them on top of the furs. "That should hold it in place." Mato gently places her on the ground, and they both go back to where they were sitting.

The temperature in the cave instantly begins to rise, and is now almost comfortable enough for the group to remove their heavy furs. Before she gets too warm, Arella decides skinning the hare she caught would be a good idea. They lay on the ground near her feet, still fluffy and not looking at all like dinner. In her absence, Maska had hunted down his own mountain hare, or two for all Arella knew, so he was not hungry. She stands, taking her dagger in hand and picks up the hare. "Do you need a hand with that?" Nootau asks.

"I think I can skin them on my own." Arella smiles. "But thanks for the offer."

"I meant your leg, not the hare." He laughs. "I still need to take a look at that."

"When I get back. We need to get some food cooked and eaten before the sun goes down." She exits the cave, taking the four hare's out into the snow.

Only twenty feet from the entrance of the cave, Arella sits on a large stone skinning the hare. This can't be done inside the cave, as the blood and guts would not be welcome there. Skinning them is quick, and there is still plenty of meat on their bones. *"These will make a nice meal."* She thinks, her stomach rumbling at the thought of juicy hare. She's only had it once before, and that was because a mountain hare must have gotten lost. It had found its way into the forest somehow, and Maska brought it home from one of his hunts.

She did not care where it came from; she only remembered that the meat was divine. They are skinned fast, and gutted just as quickly.

The cave they have chosen is situated close to the edge. Arella takes advantage of this, throwing the skins and guts over the cliff. She doesn't want to keep them too close to the cave for fear of predators.

The snow is really coming down thick, and it is hard to see the landscape around. Trees blur together, mountains and ground blend into one, all in a swirl of white snow. Arella stands in the snow, looking up at the sky above. The swirls and patterns the snow make as they fall are hypnotising. *"Beautiful."* She smiles. It really is peaceful up here, and the snow has made it warmer. She no longer shivers in the cold.*"Maybe I was born to be up here."* She bends down to the ground again, using the snow to wash the blood from her hands. The snow turns a deep red, and her hands do too, although from the cold not the blood. She wipes the snow from them, and places her dagger in her other boot, careful not to nick the skin. She then picks up the hares she had prepared, starting to freeze in the snow and starts back towards the cave, using the light of the fire as her guide. If the fire was not there, Arella is sure she would become lost in the blizzard. However beautiful it is, it is still disorientating.

Something catches her eye, and it looks to be fairly close. She squints her eyes in the dying light of the day, the glow from the sun reflecting off the white snow making it even harder to see. What she sees is a tall figure, wide and red. The shape shifts, to something equally as big but different. She recognises the shape, but it is not familiar. Then it dawns on her. It looks like the thing they saw at the top of the mountain a couple of days ago. But that was a skinwalker, and they'd got rid of all the skinwalkers in the area. Arella had made sure of that. She shakes her head, scrunching her eyes up tight as she does so. When she opens them again, the figure is gone. *"I think I need food and sleep."* She thinks, putting the mirage down to exhaustion and hunger. She then makes her way back towards the cave, finding the men all inside, toasty warm. She removes her cloak, allowing herself to warm by the fire, removes the dagger from her boot and hands Mato the hare to cook.

With the hare on the fire, Arella finally allows Nootau to look at her leg. He examines it carefully before giving his prognosis. "You've not done a bad job at stitching." He says, admiring her work. "It's a little crooked, but I don't think I could have sewn myself up like that." He touches the edge of the wound, causing Arella to jump and inhale sharply. Nashoba reacts to this.

"Careful Nootau."

"I'm okay Nashoba." Arella reassures him. "It doesn't hurt too bad." She laughs.

"What are you laughing at?" Nashoba asks.

"There you are with a spear sticking out of your chest, and you're worried about me with a cut on my leg." The others join in with the laughter.

"It really is just a scratch Nashoba." Nootau says, then turns back to Arella. "It does look angry though."

"What do you mean it looks angry? It's a cut."

"I mean it's a little infected. Needs antiseptic." Nootau explains.

"And where are we meant to get that in the mountains?" Arella asks.

"Minno mushrooms." Mato says, holding a grey/purple flowery mushroom in front of him.

"What on earth are minno mushrooms?" Arella asks, having never seen anything like them before.

"Well they're not as good as your barrow berries, but they come a close second." He explains, taking the mushroom from Mato. It is now that Arella notices the strange purple mush on Nashoba's chest. It must be the same thing. "It won't completely heal the wound, but it will take away the infection, cool it and stop it getting any worse."

"How do you know about this plant?" Arella asks.

"They used to grow close to home. There were loads of them

back home, and we used them a lot." He explains.

"Well you might have done." Nashoba says. "I never liked the idea of rubbing a mushroom into myself."

"Now look at you." Arella laughs. They all do at this. Nootau applies the mushrooms to Arella's leg, instantly cooling it and making it feel better. She sighs with relief as pain, swelling and heat almost instantly leave the wound. "That feels so much better."

"Looks it too." Nashoba smiles. Arella smiles back at him.


The hare tastes just as Arella remembers. The hot, sweet juices fill her mouth, the tender meat falling apart as she chews. She can't help but say "MMM" as she eats. She looks around at the others, all of whom are enjoying the hare as much as she is. She'd forgotten how hungry she was until the hare was cooking over the flames. The smell of cooking meat filling the air. Arella briefly thought back to the boy the other day, but quickly pushed this thought from her mind, choosing to forget it even happened. The sounds and smells from that night will haunt her dreams, but she can at least push them away while she is awake.

# Chapter 8

Arella awakens from a deep sleep. Something has woken her but she can't put her finger on it. She looks towards the entrance of the cave. The wind has blown the furs aside slightly, letting cold air into the warmth. That must have been it. She rolls over, closing her eyes and getting comfortable again. She pulls her furs up higher so they are almost covering her completely and closes her eyes again. She smiles in the dark of the cave. The sun has not yet come up, but Arella can feel it is close. *"I'll just sleep a little more. Savour the warmth of my furs before we have to get up and into the cold."* She peeks her eyes open, looking over at Nashoba laid next to her on the ground. He looks peaceful there, and not in pain at all. She looks closer at the wound on his chest, the purple mushroom paste around it looks to be working. Come to think of it, her own leg is not hurting either. *"Well done Nootau."* She closes her eyes again, breathing in deep and relaxing into her furs. Tiredness takes over her again, and the fussiness of dreams begins to swim around her.

A strange pressure on her face wakes Arella. She jumps and pulls backwards, frightened by the unwanted pressure. Her eyes open

wide and she sees Nootau's face close to hers, his index finger
pressed to his lips. Arella calms herself, slowing her heart rate down
again. *"What's wrong?"* She raises her shoulders up and down.
Nootau removes his hand from her mouth and points towards the
doorway. Arella turns, expecting to see something behind her, but
instead sees nothing. It is the nothing that is worrying. *"What is he
so worried about?"* Arella turns to look at Nootau again, confused.
Nootau simply mouths the word 'bear'.

Arella steadies herself. *"A bear?"* The panic is quite clear in her
eyes. She looks to Nashoba, still in his furs, now sitting. He looks
worried, and rightly so. Arella then looks over to Mato. The fear on
his face is clearer than day. It was a bear who scarred his face, and
although Arella does not know the full story, she knows this much.
They barely escaped with their lives, and Mato will never forget the
bear. He must be terrified, knowing that creature is out there.
Maska looks a little worried too, although Arella gets the feeling her
is feeding off the anxiety in the cave. Mato is gets his boots on
rapidly, then helps Nashoba. He really isn't in any fit state to be
fighting a bear. That leaves them one man down, and Arella isn't the
strongest. They are definitely at a disadvantage if the bear attacks.

Arella pulls her boots on quickly, attaching the dagger that cut
her to the very leg it cut. She fixed its holster the night before in the

light of the fire, strengthening it and adding extra fur for padding. In fact, she spent most of the night padding out everyone's boots with fur. They all dress quickly, storing all furs away in their animal skin bags. It's worrying to be woken up this quickly, and Arella is a little sceptical. There has been no sign of a bear since she was woken. Arella is now beginning to wonder if the bare is even real. She stands, taking her grathon in hand and walks gingerly towards the edge of the cave. Nootau grasps her thin arm, holding tight to it. She tenses her arm, the muscle becoming tight and pulls away. He's trying to stop her looking, but Arella is too curious, too suspicious. She holds the grathon tight and steps towards the entrance. She carefully pulls the furs to the side, revealing the bright white light of the snow outside. It's fallen thick, but the sky is clear now. Arella looks around. "Don't go out there." Mato whispers from behind her. Arella ignores him. She has to be the brave one. If she does not find out if there really is a bear, and get rid of it if there is, they might be stuck in that cave for a while.

On the ground outside, pressed into the fresh snow, are paw prints. These prints are big. Much bigger than Maska's, and Arella thought his paws were big. They are a different shape too, definitely not feline. The pads are large, but the claws that extend from them are even bigger. She looks around, seeing no bear in the vicinity. She bends to the paw print to inspect it further, and finds some fur in the print, embedded into the packed snow. The fur is a deep red/orange colour, and long. Arella places her hand in the print, still able to see the edges from beneath her fingers. *"Wow."* She looks around again at the forest. All is quiet, and there is no bear in sight. Nothing but the white of the snow and the deep brown of the dead trees. She looks back to the cave and sees the men all peeking from the side of the fur cover. "I think we're clear." She says to them, but their reaction worries her. They do not exit the cave, nor do they even look pleased with her answer. She knows the look on their faces, and it is not a good one. It is exactly the same look they had when the rabid wolf attacked them in the forest all those years ago. Arella swallows, her throat thick. Soft padding behind her, then deep breathing. Arella turns to find herself in the sight of the giant auburn bear.

The great bear stands up on its hind legs. If Arella thought it was big before, it is twice as big now. It must be seven foot high on its hind legs. It shakes its great muscular head, the ripples travelling down its body as it does so, shaking soft snow from its back and forearms. Snow crystals cover the bears paws, but the claws underneath are unmistakable. They are long, and sharp. The great bear opens its mouth and lets out an almighty roar, a roar big enough to shake the ground, and shake Arella to her core. She knew a bear was big, and she knew they were frightening, but she was not prepared for this. The bear then drops to all fours, shaking the ground as it lands on the snow, causing cloud of powder to come up. It roars again, this time intending on charging at Arella. Instincts take over and she lowers the grathon, angling one of the spear ends towards the bear, digging the other into the ground for balance and strength. She made the mistake with the buffalo of not anchoring herself. She will not make it again.

As the bear is charging, Arella calls back to the men and Maska. "Get out!" She shouts to them. Arella does not want them to be anywhere near if the bear gets past her, or if she fails to stop it. They need to be kept alive. They do as she tells them, leaving the cave and starting up the mountain. Nashoba stops and turns to look at Arella. The red wolf at Arella's chest grows hot. She looks back at Nashoba briefly. With everything in slow motion, Arella changes her mind about the position of the grathon. She switches it around, pulling it free from its anchor in the ground, and turning it on its side so both spear ends were to the sides. She does this so fast that the great bear has no time to adjust itself and barrels into her anyway. Arella moves fast, ducking herself and tucking around the grathon, rolling under the bear as it dives for her. The bear catches an arm on the edge of the grathon, tripping on the wood. It hits the floor face first. Nashoba throws Arella's bow to her, then the arrows, and Arella throws the grathon back to him. The bear is still on the ground, but he won't be for long. "Won't you need that?" Nashoba shouts as he catches the weapon, wincing in pain at his shoulder.

"Just run, I'm right behind you." The bear is up then, looking at the men and Maska. Arella picks up a stone from the ground and fires it at the hind quarters of the bear with her bow. She knows her arrows will not pierce its tough hide, and there is no point breaking the arrows trying. The bear turns on her, roaring loudly in her face before rearing up again. "There's a black tree up the way. I saw it last night." Arella shouts, the bear back on all fours and walking towards her menacingly. She has to keep its attention. She throws another stone, this time catching it on the shoulder. "Climb and wait for me." The stone connects with the bears shoulder, causing it to go into a fit of rage.

The men all start running, Nashoba helped by Nootau and Mato. Arella watches them leave as she keeps the bears attention. This is risky, and Arella is terrified. But with Mato having a fear of bears, Nashoba in no fit state to fight, and Nootau having to help Nashoba to run, she is the only one who can distract the beast. She moves to the side, allowing the bear to move around her. They circle each other, keeping eye contact the entire time. Arella doesn't know much about bears, but she does know that they are powerful. If it were to get hold of her, she would have no chance.

The bear rears up again, now standing in its original position. Arella now has her back towards the cave, perfect for being able to follow the others. As the bear rears up, making itself look as big as possible, it roars at her, showing her its bright white teeth. Arella copies the bear, making herself as big as she can, lifting her arms into the air and roaring back. The bear looks a little shocked at this, but simply roars back in competition. A strong gust of wind blows, knocking Arella's hood back, revealing her bright white hair and pale skin beneath. The bare stops at this sight, almost like it has never seen someone of her complexion before, which in hindsight it probably hasn't. Arella uses this shock to her advantage, turning on her heels and running away from the bear. She knows it is faster than her on the straight, but if she can use the rocks and trees, perhaps she can keep away from it long enough to get to the black tree. She does not know what it is that draws her to the tree, but she knows that they will be safe there.

With the bear following close behind, Arella must do something to keep it back. She bends as she runs, picking up a stone from the ground, and tosses it backwards at the bear. This catches it in the face, slowing it a little, but not enough. The path ahead it smooth and straight, not very good for Arella to keep the bear at bay. Up ahead she spots the others, all running and peering back over their shoulders, watching out for Arella. When they see her, the look of fear on their faces is the only thing Arella can think about. She looks around at the bear, now much closer than she originally thought it was. This is like the beast in the forest all over again, except now Arella is weaker and more tired than then, and there is no canyon to lose the bear in like there was before. She keeps on running towards her friends, towards the black tree. It is in sight now, not far away. Thoughts race through her mind as she runs. *"Why the black tree? What will we find when we get there? Will we get there before the bear gets us?"* All thoughts merge into one big ball of panic and Arella begins to get dizzy. She shakes her head, clearing the fussiness for a moment.

Suddenly something black darts past her. Its fur brushing her leg as it goes. "Maska?" Arella shouts back, still running in the direction of her friends. The great auron cat has taken it upon himself to attack the bear. *"This is madness."* Arella can't help but think. She knows he cannot take on a bear by himself, and the beast would kill him without even a second thought. She turns to see Maska dive straight for the bears face, causing it to stop and take notice of him. Once Maska has the bears attention, he keeps his distance. This is a smart move, and Maska knows what he is doing.

Arella keeps running, making some distance between her and the bear. She gets to the others before they make it to the black tree and they stop. "Climb." Arella says to the men.

"You first." Nashoba says.

"No." Arella answers. "I'm the fastest climber, so I go up last. We need everyone else up there first in case the bear comes back." Nashoba steps towards the tree. "No not you Nashoba." He looks confused at her. "We need Mato and Nootau to help lift you into the tree. You'll never get up there with that shoulder the way it is." Mato takes the lead, climbing the tree first. One foot in front of the other, he makes it into the bow of the tree. Nootau begins climbing next.

With the distraction in front of her, Arella had not noticed the bear. It's lost interest in chasing after Maska, and is once again heading straight for her and the others, straight for the safety of the black tree. She feels the ground beneath her begin to shake as the bear pounds towards them. Maska is trying his best to distract it, but the beast has lost interest. Arella looks back to Nootau, just about in the tree. He and Mato turn to take Nashoba's hands to pull him up but the bear is close. She turns to look at the bear again to see it only ten feet away.

Suddenly the ground cracks, the bear stops and Arella looks down. The snow has shifted, and the ice beneath is clearly visible. Arella is standing on ice, and the tree too. Maybe this isn't such a safe place for them to be. The bear has not noticed the ice comes forwards. As it steps on the sheet, the crack that formed beneath Arella's feet spreads to the base of the tree. "Stop!" Arella shouts, but the bear does not understand. It takes another step. The ground shakes. Arella looks around at Nashoba, his feet still on the ground, reaching up for Nootau and Mato, when all of a sudden the ice breaks.

Arella and Nashoba plummet into the depths of the ice, falling through a cave just below the tree. Arella feels the pain of the hard stone ground as she hits the floor and groans as she pulls herself up from it. As she moves away from the stone on her back, Arella hears a crack. Her bow and quiver of arrows were on her back. She pulls them free, dropping them to the ground to inspect later. Her first reaction is to look around for Nashoba, who she finds unconscious on the ground close to her. His head is bleeding, but only a little from what she can see. She also can't see anymore damage from the spear in his chest. This looks to be the same, no more blood there. And he is still breathing, so that's a bonus. Arella panics and rushes to his, lifting his head gingerly and placing it on her lap. She looks up around the rest of the cave, searching for the bear, but it is nowhere to be seen. Nor are the others. Nootau and Mato must still be safe in the tree above.

Looking up into the gaping hole in the roof of the cave, Arella can see nothing but the bright white light of the sky. Two shapes shadow the sun, casting long shadows into the cave below. "Are you okay?" Nootau's voice shouts down into the icy cave below.

"Nashoba's unconscious." Arella shouts back up. "What do I do?" It's dawned on her that she has no idea what to do with him.

"Is he bleeding?" Nootau asks.

"A little yeah."

"Just don't do anything. How bad is the bleeding?"

"There's not much." Arella says.

"Okay. Don't go anything. We're coming down." Nootau says. Arella looks around at the cave. Black stone can be seen beneath the ice. It shines and shimmers, the light from the sun reflecting down and lighting it up. Arella looks up again to see Nootau close to the edge looking down. As he moves, some snows shifts, falling down into the cave.

"Don't come down!" Arella shouts back up. "It's too dangerous. I'll find another way for us to get out when Nashoba wakes up." She looks down at his unconscious face. "Where did the bear go?"

"It ran away when the ice collapsed." Mato shouts down.

"And where's Maska?" Arella is panicking a little now. She hasn't seen him since she fell.

"He's okay. He's here, just not getting too close to the edge. I don't think he likes heights." Mato laughs.

"Neither do I." Arella shouts up, allowing herself a little laugh. Nashoba stirs at this sound, his eyes fluttering a little. "He's waking up." Arella says. "We'll move on into the cave. If we don't see you sooner, we'll meet you at the green mountain top. It wasn't too far away from where we were."

"Will you be okay?" Nootau shouts down.

"We'll be fine." She shouts back up. Nashoba looks up at her, his bright green eyes shining bright in the icy cave.

"Hi beautiful."

Now that Nashoba is awake, Arella takes time to assess her surroundings. The walls of the cave are coated in ace, and it looks like it would be impossible to climb. Good job she told Nootau and Mato not to come down. She noticed earlier that the cave seems to go a lot further up the mountain, it slowly looks to slope up, and although her view is blocked by a corner, Arella has a feeling that this is the way out of the cave. In the opposite direction, the cave slopes downwards. Is it possible that this was once an underground river? This seems like a likely explanation. That would mean that the water would have had to come from somewhere, and that is where Arella is aiming to go.

She looks over at her bow and quiver of arrows, leaving Nashoba to get himself up carefully. He does not need her help now he is awake, and encourages her to check her bow. When she gets to her weapon, Arella does not find what she was hoping for. The bow is broken clean in two, the only thing holding it together is the string. "I'm sorry." Nashoba says from behind her.

"It's okay." Arella answers back, clearly sad about her bow. "I can make another one."

"Maybe we can fix it?" Nashoba asks. Arella knows that would not be possible. She takes her arrows from the ground and inspects them too. The shafts are broken, but the bloodglass heads are still intact. That's something at least. She places them back in the quiver and pulls it onto her back, turning to look at Nashoba.

"Where's my grathon?"

"I handed it up to Nootau before I started climbing, so I wouldn't drop it." He says innocently.

"Damn." Arella curses. "Looks like we'll have to go on without it." She looks at Nashoba. He looks worried, and for good reason. They have no idea where they are, how to get to the surface, and if they will ever make it out of the cave, but they have to be strong. "At least there won't be any bears down here." Arella laughs, attempting to lighten the mood. It seems to work as Nashoba is now laughing too.

"Yeah but also no food." He smiles. It's nice to see him smile, even in times like this.


While Arella is worried about the wound on Nashoba's chest, he doesn't seem to notice it much now. With furs pulled up close around their faces to shield them from the icy cold of the snow cave, Nashoba and Arella begin their ascent up the slope, hopefully to freedom.

The ground is slippery, making walking slow. Arella feels rather exposed, not having her bow or grathon with her. It is unnerving to her, not being able to protect herself in a strange environment. She has her dagger, but this would not be effective against most of the things that could hurt them up here in the mountains. They've been walking for a couple of hours, and the tunnel is becoming more narrow. With ice on all sides, covering hard black stone, the cave in exceedingly cold. Light still beams in from above, a thin layer of ice between them and the sky above. Once or twice Arella thought about breaking the ice and climbing out, only to realise the dangers, and the realisation of what would happen. Besides the ice being too thick for her to break, she would probably be met with an avalanche of snow, ice and rock, as well as con-caving the cave. With her luck that would be a sure thing.

# Chapter 9

Icy cold air bites at Arella's fingers and face, causing her to attempt to shield them from view. This has made seeing harder, as half of her face is covered with furs. She shivers in the cold, her muscles aching from the spasms her body is forced into to stay warm. Her sides ache, and her back, and her legs from keeping upright on the ice. Watching every move she makes, Arella has to walk slowly. Her clumsiness causes her to slip several times, managing to catch herself most of the time. Nashoba keeps his balance better than her, but even he slips once or twice. Arella has to resist the urge to go to him every time he slips. It's hard, but they would be more likely to slip if they were walking together. He's better off in front, where she can keep an eye on him. Arella is constantly worried that he might go down, and that she wouldn't be able to get him back up again, or that the wound might get worse. This fear keeps her moving, and she keeps him moving.

A strong wind whistles through the ice cave from in front, confirming that the cave does reach the surface. As it blows, Nashoba, who is in front of Arella, slips on the ice beneath his feet,

falling to the ground. Arella rushes to him. "I'm okay. Just slipped."
He snaps.

"Okay, okay." Arella steps back from him. *"He seems irritable."*

"Sorry Arella, I'm just so cold and tired." Nashoba says. "Can we
rest here for a minute." He says, shivering through his teeth.

"We can't stop now. We have to get to the surface. We can build
a fire when we get up top and keep warm that way." She tries. The
temptation to curl up on the ice with Nashoba beside her and sleep
is so strong, but Arella knows that if they went to sleep down here,
cold and tired and hungry, chances are they would never wake from
that sleep.

A shadow passes above them as they speak, then another, then
another. Arella looks up to the ice roof above them. There are
figures standing above them on the ice. The fact that they are
standing on the ice confirms that Arella would not have been able to
break it. There are two men. One of them is large and tall, the other
still well-built but not nearly as tall as the first, and the third figure is
much shorted, waist height of the taller man, but looks to be on all
fours. In Arella's tired and cold state, she does not recognise them.
It's Nashoba that notices who it is on the roof. "Is that Mato and
Nootau?"

"Is it?" Arella squints up, the sun light blinding her through the
ice. One of the figures gets down on the ground and pounds his fist

against the ice. It does nothing. Arella positions herself so she can see the figures without the glare of the sun effecting her eyes. She can see Nootau's mouth opening and closing, like he's shouting, but no words are coming out. "Can you hear them?"

"No. Can you?" He asks her. Arella strains her ears, but still cannot hear anything. Then she spots some roots growing down through the ice close to the wall. The cave slopes up a little there, and there are rocks she might be able to climb on. "Give me a second." She says, walking towards the bank of rocks at the side of the cave. She starts climbing carefully on the icy rocks.

Arella reaches up to the roots and takes them in her right hand, using her left to steady herself against the wall. As she pulls, the roots come free, bringing with them dirt and snow, all falling into the cave and onto Arella. This knocks her to the ground, but thankfully there isn't much debris. She stands, rubbing her backside where it connected with the hard stone. Nashoba rushes to her, but she ensures him she's okay.

"How are you doing down there?" Nootau asks through the newly created hole. The hole is just large enough to fir an arm through, and the sound of Nootau's voice travels well.

"It's cold." Nashoba shivers. "But we're okay."

"We'll be glad when we can sit by a fire again." Arella says.

"Is there any way you can climb out here?" Nootau asks.

"I think the ice is too thick." Arella replies. "I felt a gust of wind a minute ago though coming from further up. We might be able to get out up there."

"We'll go ahead and scout it out." Mato decides. "Nootau will walk above you to keep you company." It's now clear that Mato mean himself and Maska. The auron cat will at least be able to sniff them out if they come across an entrance to the cave.

"Good idea." Arella agrees.

Mato and Maska leave, walking further up the mountain. Mato has Maska with him to protect him, and Nootau has Arella's grathon. She can see it clearly in his hand, the red bloodglass spears on both ends shimmering in the sunlight. "So what's the damage?" Nootau asks.

"Just my bow and arrows broken." Arella sighs. "No real damage to me or Nashoba." The red wolf at her chest burns hot, keeping her warmer than she should be.

"Well that's a bonus then." Nootau laughs. "You'd better get walking guys. You'll get way too cold down there if you stay overnight, and the sun will be going down in a couple of hours."

"Stay close." Arella shouts up to him."

The further through the cave they walk, the more worried she is becoming. Even if they make it out of the cave with Nashoba still okay, how much further up the mountain can he go? He's slowing now. Arella is starting to feel the pain in her leg once again, which means Nashoba must be feeling it in his chest too. She decides to check on him to make sure he's okay. "I'm fine." He snaps. This is enough of an answer for Arella. She decides to leave him alone. She will talk to Nootau and Mato when they get out of the cave. Maybe one of them can take him back home to his village, or find a way to make him better. Something has to happen though. He's getting worse the longer he's away from medicine, and Arella can't see him lasting much longer out here in the wilderness. She looks at him in front of her, a little slumped over. Worry is a constant in her heart at the moment, and it aches almost as much as her back in the cold.

After another hour of walking, slipping and trying to keep upright, Nashoba has had enough. He sits down on the ground and refuses to move. "Come on Nashoba, we have to keep going."

"I'm tired." He complains. "And cold." Mist escapes his mouth as he exhales, exaggerating the cold even more.

"But we have to keep going." Arella urges. "We won't be far from the end of the cave now." She moves to sit next to him. "Mato and Nootau will have a fire for us when we reach the surface, and we can get warm again. Maska will hunt us some food, and then we can take a look at your chest. Make sure the wound is not getting worse." Nashoba looks defeated. It hurts Arella to see him this way.

He looks smaller somehow, younger, like a child. Her heart aches for him. Arella has literally taken him away from his family and brought him into the wilderness, taken him into a dangerous world, got him hurt, almost killed, cold, hungry and exhausted, now she's telling him he has to keep going. He looks like he's about to give up, and Arella is going the same way. Her eyes were fluttering as she was walking, almost falling asleep as she walked.

Arella takes a seat next to Nashoba on the icy ground. *"A couple of minutes won't do us any harm."* She thinks as she seats herself down, taking the weight off her back. It's starting to get darker now, and the temperature is dropping rapidly. Arella can see her breath in front of her face, and feel the ice biting at all exposed flesh. Her leg is really aching too. She can't stand much more time in here. Arella's breathing becomes shallow and heavy, her heart rate increases, she gets hot and sweaty, a sick feeling in the pit of her stomach. She's panicking now, thoughts racing through her mind. *"What if we never get out?" "What if the cave collapses with us inside?" "What if we die here?"* The thoughts are coming through thick and fast. Nashoba spots her panic and goes to her, placing steady hands on her shoulders.

"Arella calm down." He says to her in a soothing voice. He's panicking just as much as she is, but he can't let her see.

"But we're going to be stuck down here forever." She panics, her eyes filling with tears.

"Don't say that. We're going to get out." Nashoba doesn't sound too sure, and Arella can hear this in his voice. Arella begins to sob.

"I've brought you here." She cries. "I've brought you to a dangerous place you didn't need to come to. I got you hurt. I caused you pain, and now you're stuck in a cave with me, waiting to die." The tears are flowing freely now.

"Stop that now Arella." Nashoba stops her, holding her shoulders tighter as if he is trying to hold her together himself. "I came up to the mountains with you because I saw; no I see something in you." She looks up at him, teary purple eyes shining bright and wet. "Arella I'm going to tell you something I've not said out loud before." He looks at her, his green eyes intense. "I love you Arella." Her heart almost stops. The tears stop almost instantly.

"You what?" She asks, not believing that he really said it.

"I love you, you strange girl." He says again. Arella practically leaps into his arms, hugging him tight. He winces in pain as she presses against the wound on his chest.

"Oh, sorry." She pulls away quickly.

"It's okay." He smiles. He then sits next to her on the rock. She closes her eyes for a second, letting the darkness calm her. She slows her heart rate and breathes deep. *Come on Arella. You can do it.* Just then, a noise makes her jump. The sound of scratching on ice, then heavy breathing. She opens her eyes suddenly and looks at Nashoba. He too is looking back at her with his green eyes, wide in fear. "The bear?" Arella mouths, not wanting to make a sound. The scratching continues, so does the breathing. Arella's heart rate is rising again.

Arella stands from her seated position, taking her dagger from her boot. If it is the bear coming back for more, she's going to be ready for it. Arella stands from her seated position, taking her dagger from her boot. If it is the bear coming back for more, she's going to be ready for it.

Arella steps forwards and peeks around the corner where the noise is coming from. There is now banging as well as the scratching and heavy breathing. She noticed that the cave ends here and her heart both sinks and rejoices. On the one hand, they will not be able to get out here, but on the other, the bear will not be able to get in to get them either. She moves another step forwards. "Arella what are you doing?" Nashoba questions why she would move towards the noise.

"Something's not right." She says, listening to the noises coming from the wall. She strains her ears.

"They must be in here."

"Can we even get through. The ice seems really thick."

"Come on Maska can smell them. We have to get through to

them." The voices are faint, but Arella know them.

"Nashoba it's them!" She shouts excitedly, turning to him. "They're on the other side of this wall?" He stands and walks towards her, tired but excited.

"Well we have to get to them then. We have to get out of here." He says.

Both Arella and Nashoba rush to the wall, picking up anything they can find, smashing it against the ice, scraping it down, trying desperately to get through to the other side. Mato lifts a rock up high from the other side, smashing it into the wall with all high might. The wall cracks, and some of the ice chips away, leaving a small berry sized gap in the wall. Some ice from above rains down on Arella and Nashoba, dusting them with the fine crystals. "Stop!" Arella shouts. They all do so instantly. She looks at the wall, a crack has appeared from the small hold Mato's rock made. It stretches all the way down to the floor, and up to the roof. On closer inspection, it would appear that the crack has spread onto the roof also. This is where the ice came raining down from. "Guys we have a small issue." Arella says. Her voice can now be clearly heard through the wall.

"What, what's wrong?" Nootau's voice sounds through the wall, a little echoed but still clear.

"The roof has cracked as well as the wall." Arella explains. "If we break the wall, the roof might cave in."

"What other choice do we have?" Mato asks. Arella thinks for a minute.

"None. We have to break it anyway, just be careful." She says finally.

"Okay, stand back then." Mato says. Arella and Nashoba take a couple of steps back from the wall, and Mato continues to pound away at it, slowly chipping away at more and more of the ice wall.

With each piece of ice that chips away from the wall, the roof becomes weaker and weaker. Arella takes another step backwards, and Nashoba follows her. With one mighty blow, Mato knocks clean through the ice, shattering it, letting the dim orange light of the setting sun stream through. The light is initially blinding, and Arella is dazed by this. She pauses in the cave, now free to leave but unable to move. "Come on Arella, let's get out before the place collapses." Nashoba's voice sounds next to her. He takes hold of her hand, pulling her in the direction of the opening.

As they leave their icy prison, the whole thing collapses behind them. They barely made it out before ice, snow and rock came caving in on each other. "Phew." Nootau says as they step away from the fallen rocks. "Glad we got you out of there when we did."

Arella immediately runs to them, hugging them as tightly as she can. She then turns to Maska, hugging him also. "Thank you for getting us out guys. It was awful in there." She shivers.

"I think we need to get a fire going, get you warm." Nootau says, looking at both Nashoba and Arella who are shivering violently.

"But we're exposed." Nashoba questions. "There is nowhere to camp up here that would be sheltered. What if the bear comes back?"

"We'll take turns sleeping. That way one of us will always be awake." Nootau suggests. They all agree that this is a good idea.


Arella helps with the search for branches. Luckily, most of the trees this far up the mountain are already dead. The bad news in this is of course that from tonight, they will have no more trees to burn to keep warm at night. Arella pushes this thought from her mind. She will chose to worry about it when she is warm again, and when Nootau has had chance to look at Nashoba's chest.


Maska has been sent off hunting, and will hopefully come back with something nice. He left not long ago, but Arella is already feeling separation anxiety from him not being around. She is constantly looking for him. She places the branches on the ground, and Mato begins building the fire up and lighting it. The sky is now almost dark, making lighting the fire much harder, but he manages it. The flames roar into life, lighting up the area around them.

They've chosen a camp-site not too far away from the collapsed entrance to the cave. It is almost completely surrounded by high rocks, with only one side exposed. This means it will be easier to spot the bear if it comes back.

Nootau is inspecting Nashoba's chest when Maska comes back. He is dragging a small deer with him, pulling it along the floor with all his effort. It must have been heavy to drag all the way back here. "The wound hasn't gotten any worse." Nootau says while inspecting the red wolf's chest. "The mushrooms are still working, just not taking the pain away anymore. I grabbed a handful before we left the cave. Let me see if I can find some." He says, getting up from the ground.

Arella lazily strokes Maska's soft fur as she watches the scene unfold around her. Everything seems so normal now. Nootau is crushing more mushrooms to cover Nashoba's wound, Maska is purring softly next to her, the fire is burning bright, keeping them warm, and Mato is preparing the deer to be cooked. After everything they have been through, Arella can really say that she has found her soul mates, her best friends, and the people she wants to be around her for the rest of her life. She smiles to herself, looking up at the stars. The sky changes before her eyes. It begins to swirl in bright greens and blues, dancing slowly above her.

"Beautiful." She says. The others all look up at the sky too. It must be a sign from the spirits. They're close now. So close.

# Chapter 10

That night was pretty uneventful. Nootau tended to wounds, they ate the deer Maska brought back to the camp, and took turns on lookout while the others slept. Arella struggles to get to sleep initially, but woke feeling a little more refreshed. Her back was sore from sleeping on the hard stony ground, but as least she was warm. Nashoba is worrying her again though. When he woke this morning, standing from the furs and putting on his top, Arella noticed that the wound on his chest was becoming worse. Small thin lines of deep purple were spreading from the wound. When asked about it, he simply said he felt fine. That was the mushroom paste talking though. Its taking all the pain away from the wound, and making Nashoba feel better. Arella suggested to Nootau that it might be a good idea to take him back down the mountain, back to the village where they could see to the wound and get him fixed up. He agreed that this would be best, but that Nashoba would not have it. "I asked him last night if he would go back to the village to get seen to." Nootau said.

"And what did he say?"

"He said he's rather die up here on the mountain that let you go it alone." Nootau frowned. "And to be honest, I think I can speak for all of us when I say we would do the same."

This answer did not settle Arella, but she has no choice but to simply go along with it. The men she has befriended are far too stubborn to listen to her, and quite frankly, she would not want to be up here on her own either.

Once everyone is awake, the group finish off the deer from the night before. It was skinny, and there wasn't much meat on it, but still enough for four hungry people, and with some left over for the morning. With someone being awake all night long, the fire kept going. This was no easy task. The trees this high up the mountain are few and far between and looking further up there are practically none. They will not have a fire tonight when they sleep. Not unless they take firewood with them. Arella makes a mental note to collect some wood before they leave to climb higher. Arella warms her hands by the fire, the last time they will be warm in a while, and begins preparing herself for the long walk ahead. She can see the green on the top of the mountain from here, but believes they will still have to camp another night before they reach it. She pulls on her fur lined boots. They were warming by the fire, and her feet tingle with the new found heat. The others all have fur inside their boots now too. This will help prevent frostbite or numbness. Arella then tucks her trousers into the top of her boots, leaving no skin exposed, and slots her bloodglass dagger into the fur pocket on her right leg, safe and sound in case she needs it. She then picks up the long piece of paloa skin and wraps it first around her neck, then tucks it into her shirt. Putting on her cloak is the last thing she does, slotting her arms into the warm sleeves and pulling up the hood. She is instantly warmer, and feeling comfortable.

All of the spare furs are already in one of the bags, now considerably smaller seen as though they are all wearing more furs. Maska is the only one without any spare furs, but he seems to be coping just fine with the cold. Arella had told him to let her know if he was getting chilly, but he has not indicated that as yet. With her grathon in hand, and broken bow and arrows in the deerskin bag on her back, Arella and the others set out up the mountain once again.

The weapons the men brought with them were lost somewhere up the mountain, although none of them can recall when. This again leaves them short, and all members of the group are on edge because of this. They know for sure that there are wolves and bears this far up the mountain, and are not sure what else they might encounter. Tension is high in the group, and as a result there is very little conversation between them. Arella is at the head of the group, testing the ground beneath her as she walks, her faithful auron cat by her side, while the others trail behind.

Everyone is on edge, keeping an eye out for the bear, but so far they have not seen it. In fact, they have not seen anything for a while. The mountain is becoming steeper, and the only one finding it easy work is Maska. He's jumping from rock to rock, enjoying the freedom of the mountain. He's now a good fifty feet or so away from the group, playing in the snow. Arella laughs at him. It's like watching the kitten she brought up again. *If only he had a butterfly to play with.* She smiles at the auron cat. He looks back down at her, delight in his eyes. They twinkle in the bright light of the winter sun.

Behind her, Arella can hear the men talking. She does not want it to seem as though she is listening, so she simply pushes her hood back behind her ears, un-muffling the sound, and quietens the crunching footsteps on the snow.

"How far is it to the green?" Nashoba asks.

"We saw it from where we were camped last night." Nootau answers.

"But this is taking a long time to get there." Nashoba complains. Arella can tell he is getting tired. She'll suggest a break soon. "I don't know if I'm going to make it to the top guys." It's hard for Arella not to turn around and take him in her arms, hold him tight and say he'll be just fine.

"You'll make it Nashoba." Mato says. "You have to."

"I'm just so tired guys." He says, the sleepiness clear in his voice. Arella can feel the thickness coming in her throat, the strange tightness in her chest, and the pain that follows. Tears begin to well in her eyes. "*I will now cry.*" She urges herself. Digging her fingernails into her palms lessens the feelings in her chest, but they do not go completely. She pushes harder, and warmth pools in her palm. Only then does the pain in her chest and water in her eyes subside.

"We'll stop here for a little while." She says, her throat still thick but her voice holding strong.

"We can keep moving." Nashoba tries.

"We need to take a small break. I'm going to scout ahead." She says again. "I won't be long. Catch your breath, rest a little and stay safe." Arella turns to Maska and shouts him. Her voice echoes in the mountain, carrying a lot further than she thought it would. The strange eyed cat comes to her almost instantly. "I need you to stay with them. Stay close, and warn them if anything comes." She commands. The auron cat listens, moving to lie down close to the men.

"What about you?" Mato asks as he helps Nashoba to sit on a rock. "What if something comes for you?"

"I have my grathon." She says. "And besides, I don't think there is anything else up here." She turns to leave, a small drop of red falls from her hand, her finger nails still deep in the skin. Only Maska notices, but does not let on to the others.

Arella climbs over a boulder in front of her, sliding down the other side, using her left hand as a guide down and landing with a dull thump on the other side. She turns to look behind, checking that the group can no longer see her and spots her own blood on the snow. She looks down at her palms. Only the right has drawn blood, but the left has bruised a deep purple. "Damn." She says out loud. Arella knows that if the others see this they will question it. She does not want them to know she is worried about Nashoba, and she will not let them see her blood. She will not let them see her weak.

Pulling a strip from her own shirt, Arella splits it in two, then tires it around both palms. This will do two things. The first is it will hide the blood, the marks and stop it getting infected or sore, and the other is it will keep her hands warm and give her better grip on the rocks. The latter is the story she will tell the men if they notice.

With her grathon strapped to her back, and the sticks she collected back with the men, Arella can move freely up the mountain. She climbs the difficult way, liking the feeling on her hands on the rocks, both sharp and cold, but natural. She climbs for a couple of minutes, enjoying the fresh air and space. However nice it is to have company; the mood in the group recently has been very down. She can't help but feel that their quest is pointless when she is with them. It takes some space for Arella to see clearly again.

Perched on a rock at the top of the world, well not quite but the feeling is the same, Arella takes off the red wolf necklace. She sits, her hood pulled up, looking out over the world below. The trees back at her home now have a slight dusting of snow, and the lake looks to be freezing on the edges. Arella always loved how her home looked in the snow, but she is quickly becoming tired of the cold on the mountain. She turns the wolf around in her hand, letting the warm stone cool in the air. She looks down at the wolf, for the first time in real detail. She never noticed its features before, the way the eyes look alive, the way the fur seems to move as you turn it, and the heat. It never dawned on her before, but stone should not be warm. It really meant something for Nashoba to give her this wolf, and Arella has nothing to give him. The wolf is a symbol of Nashoba's heart. It is like he's given it to her to keep, to look after, to cherish, and all she's given him is a hole in his chest. This thought is a constant in her mind, and the feeling is getting her down. Instead of letting it eat away at her, Arella decides to vow something instead. She vows that she will get them all safely to the green at the top of the mountain, seek out the help of the mountain spirit, ask him to save Nashoba, then take them home again where they will be safe. "This is my new mission." She says out loud to herself. "I know who I am. I am Arella."

Putting the wolf back around her neck, Arella stands on the rock she was perched and looks down towards the men. She can see them from up here, but there is no way they can see her. She is hidden by too many rocks, and the pale colour of her lyron furs camouflage her in the snow. They are all still sat down there, the same as they were when Arella left to climb the mountain, left to think. Another thought crosses her mind. *"I could go now, up the mountain, bring the spirit down here. It would be faster than taking them up with me."* She pauses in thought for a moment. *"But then who is to say that the spirit would come with me. No I must get them up to the top, to the green. Then everything will be okay."* Arella is holding onto this hope.

She leaves her perch and heads back down to the group. "I've found a way up, but it's going to be single file some of the way." Arella says as she reaches the camp. "We'll have to be careful, but I've seen a flat area we could camp at tonight, then we can make it to the green tomorrow." They all agree that this is a good idea. "Maska, can you follow my tracks to where I just came from? Scout out ahead and see if you can find food for tonight?" She asks the auron cat. His response is to start padding away in the direction

Arella came from. Maska does not need to use words. He and Arella understand each other perfectly.

This section of the walk gets more dangerous. Once they get past the place Arella rested at, they find that the path narrows considerably. With high cliffy walls on one side, and a steep drop developing on the other, walking is perilous. There is still a good four foot from the wall to the drop, but when walking on slippery ice, this does not allow for much falling space. Moving is slow here, and Arella travels at the front of the group, checking for weak points on the path. Maska has moves on ahead, having no trouble with the ice and thin path, and is assumed to be hunting further up the mountain.

A strong gust of wind blows, making it hard to breath. Arella stops, and the others stop behind her. She shields her face from the winding, catching her breath and steadying herself. Once the wind drops again, she starts moving once again up the mountain. There is very little talking on this leg of the climb, and Arella can't help but look back at Nashoba for most of the walk. He is becoming pale, and is wincing a lot. Arella's leg is not really causing her many problems now, but his chest must be agony.

They continue up the mountain and reach the point that Arella has singled out at their final camping spot before the sun falls behind the mountain. "It's getting dark. We'd better make camp." The area she has chosen is wider than the rest of the path. A cave set into the mountain, with a large overhang and plenty of space for five. The men enter the cave, escaping the howling wind that batters the tops of the mountains. Snow has started to fall again, making the sky even darker. Arella works on building a fire in the centre of the cave, leaving room behind for her and the men to sleep, but the wind is too strong, blowing the fire out every time she creates a spark. "Gods damn it!" She shouts. She's losing her cool now, her temper flaring.

"Arella calm down." Nootau sooths. "It's okay, just keep trying."

"I'm going to find something to keep the fire going." She says without looking at anyone, furious at herself for not being able to make a fire. She leaves the cave before anyone has a chance to stop her.

# Chapter 11

A little further along the narrow path, Arella comes across something strange. It's a tree. Now I know that doesn't sound very strange, but this far up the mountain, when she has not seen another living thing all day, a tree is pretty spectacular. With the snow falling lightly around her, and a slight breeze in the air, Arella is feeling relaxed again. The weather has calmed down, and so has she. Arella has rounded a corner, meaning the wind can no longer attack her, and this makes her current job a whole lot easier. She moves to the base of the tree and begins searching. She's looking for anything she can use to shield the fire when she comes across the. A pile of large flat stones. She brushes the snow from the top of them, then picks one it. It is surprisingly light for a stone, and she picks up another, then another. *"Three should do it."*

A cawing noise catches her attention as she picks up the stones. It makes her jump. Arella instinctively looks up into the tree where the noise was coming from. Upon closer inspection, she can see that there is now one crow in the tree but about a dozen. A second crow caws, a shrill and nasty noise. Arella never likes crows, and these are just ominous. *"What would a bunch of birds be doing up here, with no food to eat and nowhere safe to nest?"* Another crow caws. The noise is unnerving, and Arella thinks it might be best if she leaves the tree, heading back to the cave they will camp in tonight.

As she starts walking away, one of the crows takes flight and lands in front of her on the cliff face. It caws at her. Its beady black eyes staring at her, unblinking. Arella lowers her head and keeps moving. This bird is really making her nervous. As she walks, more and more of the crows follow her, the cawing getting louder and louder. Arella's heart is beating faster, adrenalin rushing through her veins. She takes flight herself, running back down the thin track in low light, fresh snow the only thing stopping her from slipping on the ice beneath her feet.

With the cave in sight, the crows dive on Arella. One pecks at the back of her head, catching her hood with its beak and nicking the top of her head. The others follow suit, all dive bombing her one after another, taking turns at attacking her, all while cawing noisily.

"What in the name of the gods is that?" Mato asks, peeking his head out of the cave to see what the commotion is. He sees Arella running for her life, followed by a blackness, rocks in her arms and panic on her face. He quickly stands, bringing Nootau with him.

"What the…" Nootau is stopped in his tracks.

Arella hits a patch of ground where the snow has not yet laid, her foot slipping from under her. She flails her arms, the rocks flying forwards and landing on the ground. With her feet no longer firmly planted on the ground, Arella goes down. She's dangerously close to the edge now, and the crows are not giving up. They dive for her again. Arella uses her hands to cover her head, but this is a mistake. The crows dive on her, pecking at her hands now. They break the skin a couple of times, and still do not give up. Every time Mato or Nootau try to get to her, the crows attack them too. They simply stand there and watch the crows dive, again and again. Arella cries out for help, but they cannot get to her.

Out of nowhere, a loud roar sounds. Maska has returned from hunting and is furious to see Arella being attacked, he runs at the crows, but makes little difference to them. They dive bomb him also, and he is forced to back off.

The crows attacks seem to be less frequent, and Arella uses this to her advantage. She plants a foot under herself and pushes forwards, standing up and moving towards the cave. She slips on the ice again, and this time does not land safely on the ground. She slips further, her feet falling from the cliff. She is now hanging from the cliff, holding on with her bloody hands, still being attacked by the crows, if anything more so now than before.

Mato tries to get to her once again, but a crow takes a liking to him, going directly for his face. It catches his lip, causing it to bleed, then comes back again for a second go. Mato knocks it to the side with a strong fist, and he himself slips on a patch of ice. He gets his footing again, but is not able to get to Arella. Nashoba is still in the cave, no energy to move, but sadness on his face. He is powerless to do anything but sit there and watch the scene unfold in front of him.

Nashoba spots something in the distance, something big and dark. It's coming towards them. "Watch out!" He shouts, pointing at the shape moving towards them at speed. An eagle cry sounds in the night, and the giant beast swoops down on the crows. Its large brown wings stretch out far, and with as much grace as you'd expect from an eagle, the giant bird takes a crow in each talon and crushes them, dropping them into the abyss below. The crows stop attacking Arella and Mato, and instead turn their attention to the eagle assailant. The giant bird swoops around several times, taking out more and more of the black crows as it does.

As soon as the crows are out of the way, Nootau and Mato rush to Arella, both taking an arm each. They make sure they are anchored on the ground safely before pulling her up. Arella instantly turns to watch the eagle take out the crows. It flies away from the mountain side, and every few seconds, another black shape falls from the sky. After a little while, the crows all retreat, what's left of them anyway. "Thank you!" Arella shouts after the great eagle. She has no idea where it came from, but she sure is thankful for it being there.

Mato retrieves the rocks Arella dropped on the ground and brings them inside the cave where Arella is already sitting. She has untied the bindings around her hands and it tying them again. "Do you want me to take a look at that?" Nootau asks.

"No they're okay. Just small scratches." Arella reassures him. They hurt like hell, but there is no way she will admit it to them.

Mato places the rocks around the sticks Arella built up into a fire then lights it. The flames burst into life, brightening up the cave and warming it quickly. "How did you know the rocks would work?" He asks.

"It was just a guess." Arella says. "Something to stop the wind blowing it out."

Maska enters the cave now, bringing with him a meagre two mountain hares. From the looks of him however, he has already eaten. Two hare will do for the four of them. Arella really doesn't know what they would do without Maska. He's the only thing keeping them alive up here on the mountain. She knows people can go weeks without eating. But with spirits and energies so low, the only think keeping them going is the food Maska brings home for them every day.

Once the fire is lit, Mato works on skinning, gutting and cooking the hare. Maska has resumed his position next to Arella, and she is seated next to Nashoba, her hand on his lap and head on his shoulder. She is so tired. "So what did you do to anger the crows?" Nashoba asks. The vibrations of his chest as he talks are soothing to her.

"I don't know." She replies. "I took the rocks from under a tree, and suddenly they were there."

"They weren't sacred rocks were they?" Nootau asks.

"Nothing special about them from what I could see." Mato says.

"No I couldn't see anything either." Arella says. "They just started following me, then diving at me." She shivers. "If it wasn't for that eagle I don't know what would have happened." She admits.

Once the hare is cooked and eaten, it does not take long for Mato and Nootau to fall asleep. It never does. Maska is also snoring away, laid on his back, legs in the air as he normally does. Only Arella lies awake, next to Nashoba on the ground. She thinks he's asleep too. His chest rises and falls slowly. Arella just lies there, on the ground of the cave, fire burning warm, staring at Nashoba. "We'll get you to the mountain Nashoba. I promise we'll get you there, and when we do, the mountain spirit will make you better again."

"How can you be sure?" He asks. Arella was not expecting him to be awake.

"I just am." She says, determination in her voice. "I'm not letting you dies Nashoba. I will make you better, if its the last thing I do." Arella then rolls over to sleep.

"I hope so." Nashoba says. He too then rolls over to sleep, mincing at the pain in his chest as he does.


Arella had trouble sleeping that night. Every time she would drop off, she would hear the cawing of crows. Arella would open her eyes to find the beasts making the noise, only to be met with the dim fire, cave and night sky outside. The snow has stopped falling again, and bright stars once again fill the sky. Other noises fill the small dreams Arella manages to fall into. She dreams of being chased by a bear, but the bear is no ordinary bear. It kills the others outright, ripping them apart. When the bear finally gets to Arella, it is covered in the blood of her friends. The bears comes close to her, but does not kill her straight away. Instead it transforms in to human, but not just any human. The bear turns into Arella herself, but different. She is herself but with dark brown hair and reddish brown skin. Her eyes are no longer the bright violet she has grown to love, but a soulless black, empty and dark. Nightmare Arella walks forwards, laughing at the pale girl in front of her, before extending an arm. The nightmare Arella picks the real Arella up by the throat, strangling her, squeezing all of the life from her, all the while repeating a line that has been haunting Arella's days as well as nights. Something she has been telling herself ever since Nashoba got hurt. "This is all your fault."

When morning breaks, and the light of the sun can be seen from behind the mountain, Arella sighs. She has had practically no sleep, and does not feel refreshed in the slightest. She is first up, poking at the fire to get the last remnants of life from it. The others soon wake up, and they dress ready for their hopefully final day in the snow. As Nashoba pulls his furs back, the wound on his chest is visible. It looks angry, purple and sore. "Nootau do we have any of those mushrooms still?" Arella asks, not taking her eyes from the wound on Nashoba's chest, the blood soaked wood still sticking out from the hole.

"Yeah, in my bag, but there's not much now." He answers.

"I'm okay Arella, I don't need it." Nashoba tries.

"Yes you do." Arella urges. "Just for today, then we can make you better again. The mountain spirit will make you better." Arella is willing this to happen. Maybe if she wishes for it enough, it will come true. The mountain spirit will be at the top of the mountain, in the green, where life grows at the edge of the earth, and he will heal Nashoba, he will make him better. He has to. Nashoba looks at her face, the sadness and determination in her purple eyes.

"Okay." He gives in. He sits back down on the ground while Nootau applies the last of the crushed mushrooms. It is clear from his face that they give him instant relief. Every muscle in his face relaxes, the pain leaving his eyes, his shoulders relaxing and lowering. The wound is really taking its toll on Nashoba.

Once the group have packed up again, they continue up the mountain.

Chapter 12

Arella and the group come across the tree she collected the stones from the night before. Mato decided that it might be best if they put the rocks back where Arella found them, just in case there was a reason they were there, and a reason the crows attacked. "They don't look any different." Arella said as she places them on the ground where she found them.

"Maybe not, but there might be something about them." Nootau replies. "Best to put them back anyway. It saves us getting attacked again by the crows."

"Not that there are many of them left now." Nashoba laughs. The mushroom paste has made him happier than normal, a little giddy.

"Well I won't be taking rocks from the ground now without checking for crows first." Arella promises.

"I think that goes for all of us." Mato says, licking his lip where the crow caught it.

Looking at the tree in daylight, there is nothing strange about it. The branches flow in the same way as any other tree, and there are no leaves on it. This is to be expected, seen as though they are at the top of a mountain covered in snow and ice. The only strange thing about this lone tree is that it is here. It has grown on solid rock, where the air is thin and there is no warmth to help it grow. The tree is large, so it must have been here hundreds of years, maybe even more. Arella decides that they should move on from the tree as a shiver runs down her spine.

The path up the mountain soon widens again, making walking much easier. With freshly fallen snow on the ground, the ice is covered, meaning there is less risk of slipping. Maska is scouting ahead, checking that the group will be able to traverse the mountainside. He has been gone a couple of minutes, when he returns with a look of confusion on his face. "What have you found?" Arella asks. She turns to look at the others, but they look just as confused as she does. "Show me Maska." The auron cat turns on his heels and walks back in the direction he came, the whole group following.

They round a corner and a sound can be heard. It echoes through the mountains, and suddenly Arella is hit with the notion that she did not hear it sooner. It is like thunder, deep and booming in the mountains. The others can hear it too, but they do not know what it is. "What is that?" Nootau asks as they walk, cocking his head to the side to listen better. Arella turns to look at the men. She is met with Nootau's skinny face. He's lost weight since they started on the journey. He still has his muscles, but his cheek bones are now visible beneath his skin. He has bags under his eyes also from the lack of good sleep, but his eyes are bright with excitement.

The next person Arella focuses on is Mato. His big frame seems even bigger now that Nootau's has shrunken. He has not lost any of his mass, but he looks older. Perhaps it could be the added dirt on his face, making the scar that covers it look all that much bigger, or maybe it's the scratches on his face from the crows. He doesn't look as excited as Nootau, but more nervous. For someone who is named after a bear, and for someone who is normally as brave and strong as a bear, this journey is taking it out of him.

The last person Arella looks at is Nashoba. Beautiful Nashoba. Arella thinks he is still beautiful, but some of that has been lost. He is not himself at the moment, lost in his own world. This is partly because of the mushroom paste, but Arella fears it may also be the infection spreading. It is clear just from looking at the wound on his chest, the end of the spear still sticking out from his skin, the colour the stone has turned the longer it is embedded in his flesh. It started out a pale grey, although stained with Nashoba's blood. It now however is an angry purple. He is not looking at Arella, but instead staring into the sky. Arella follows his gaze, and so do the others. There is a shape in the sky, a large bird. It is black against the sky, and Arella's first thought is that it's one of the crows that came for her last night. She initially panics, then regains herself when she realises what it truly is. The wings are much bigger than that of a crow, and as the sun catches it, she sees that it is not black, but a golden brown. This must be the eagle that saved them last night. She silently thanks it again before bringing her eyes back down on her friends.

"It's a river." Arella finally says.

"A river this high up?" Nootau asks. "How is that even possible?"

"Well water travels down right?" Mato says, almost like it is the only reason there could be a river this high.

"Well yeah I know that." Nootau laughs. "I mean, a stream I could understand, but a river?"

"It doesn't matter why it's up here." Arella interrupts. "Let's just hope we don't have to cross it to get to the green." The others consider this for a moment.

"I'm not a good swimmer." Mato says, moving his left foot back and forth on the ground in embarrassment. "And I don't think Nashoba is in any fit state to swim anywhere." He looks at the green eyed wolf, still staring at the eagle in the sky and giggling to himself, pointing periodically.

"We'll figure it out." Arella says. "We should at least go check it out before we start panicking about how to get across. It might not be as big as it sounds. Noise echoes in the mountains remember?"

Arella looks down at the chasm below. She can see water falling, and there looks to be a lot of it. The others spot this to, but no one mentions it. As they round another corner, it becomes clear that the river is not small, but a raging torrent of white water. The sight in front of them is truly beautiful. White water falls from a higher point on the mountain, causing a waterfall to cascade down the mountain. This waterfall then drops down into a river, which seems to flow off the edge of the mountain itself. *"I bet this river eventually flows into the lake at home."* Arella walks close to the river, to the edge where it drops off again down the mountain. It looks like if falls forever, into nothingness. The group are higher than the clouds now, and the river is flowing into those clouds.

Around the river the waterfall has created, life blooms everywhere. There is grass on the ground, soft and green, flowers grow in the cracks of the mountainside and along edges. Even a few trees can be seen, and although they are spindly and thin, they are still growing. It is amazing that anything is growing this high up. It is beautiful, a paradise at the top of the mountain.

The water looks crisp and clean. The temptation to just strip off and just in is huge. Arella feels dirty, and would give anything to be able to get into the water and swim around. She moves to the water's edge, bending to the water and kneeling next to it. She removes her cloak, exposing her bare arms underneath, and plunges her hands into the cold water. It is icy cold, but amazingly refreshing. She looks at her reflection in the water. Her face is covered in mud, blood and gods know what else. Her hair is matted and no longer the beautiful pale blond it used to be, but stained with dirt and grime, knotted and matted beyond belief. This makes her want to get into the water even more. Arella looks around at the river and realises the water is hardly moving in front of her. It is slow and deep. The sun is high in the sky, and she could really do with a bath. It might do the others good too. She makes a rash decision and decides to tell the others. "I think we should camp here tonight."

"But it's still early afternoon." Nootau says. "Why do you want to camp here?"

"I figure that seen as though we're not far from the top, and there's water and life here, we should stay here for the night. I will go ahead and scout out, see just how far it is to the green, then tomorrow we continue there." She explains.

"Why don't we just keep going until we get there, and do that tonight?" Mato asks.

"We all need a break. Look at us." She says, gesturing to herself.

"We're all tired, dirty and in need of a good night's sleep. Plus I don't want to get to the green as the sun is going down. We need to have our wits about us in case there is anything up there that might harm us." The others all think about this for a little while, then agree.

"First thing's first." Arella smiles. "I need a bath." Her cloak is already off, so the next thing to remove are her boots. Arella sits on the ground and takes them off, revealing her feet to the world. She then turns to look at the men, who are all staring at her in disbelief.

"You're going to get into that water? It looks freezing." Nashoba says.

"Have you seen yourselves recently guys?" Arella laughs. "You don't exactly look pleasant, and neither do I. I really need this bath. Cold or not." She places her hands on the bottom of her shirt and lifts, slightly exposing her midsection. "Erm... Guys." She blushes. They all instantly look away. Arella quickly removes her top and trousers, then jumps into the water, dive-bombing in, making a huge splash as she goes. She comes up for air a few seconds later, her hair now dripping wet. "Oh gods this feels nice." She smiles, leaning her head back into the water, rubbing her hair until it feels smooth again.

She looks over at the men again, all still facing away from her. A sudden surge of confidence fills her up. "I can't honestly be the only one in need of a bath." She shouts over to them. "Come on in Maska." She says to the auron cat. He doesn't need to be told twice. The black auron cat slowly slinks into the water and swims over to Arella. She forgot how much the cat liked the water, and it is clear from the shining in his eyes that he thoroughly enjoys the feeling of water in his fur. "What about you guys?" She asks the men. Nashoba turns a little towards her, but keeps his eyes averted.

"We'll wait for you to get out." He says. Almost before he's finished his sentence, Nootau is undressed and dive-bombing into the river too. He comes up a second later.

"I wouldn't wait for her to get out." He laughs. "I was starting to itch I was getting so dirty." It was always clear that Nootau was the most confident of the group, and to jump into the river completely stark naked in front of everyone, especially Arella, takes guts. She managed to look away just as his trousers came down. She's close with the men, she might even call them brothers now, but she does not want to see Nootau or Mato naked. Nashoba however is a different matter. She wouldn't mind seeing him without any clothes on.

Mato is next to jump into the water. He is not quite as confident as Nootau, but once Arella turns around so he can get into the water, he joins them. Nashoba however is reluctant to get in.

"What's wrong?" Arella asks him, swimming to the edge to meet him. Maska is now out of the water, drying himself by the side, and Nootau and Mato and splashing each other like children.

"I just don't want to get my chest wet." Nashoba says finally.

"So just get in up to waste height." Arella says. "The water is more shallow at the side." Nashoba eventually agrees to get into the water, but only if Arella turns away. She does so, and Nashoba gingerly walks into the water. Once he is submerged enough to allow Arella to look at him, he tells her she can turn around. The wound on Nashoba's chest is looking worse every time Arella sees it. "*I hope the mountain spirit will help us.*" She thinks again.

Arella swims around for a minute or two in the cold water, stretching aching muscles and soothing all her pains. She can feel fish in the water, brushing past her as she swims. Her first thought is that they will make a good meal for that night, and her second is how on earth she is going to catch them. Then again, Arella has never had trouble catching fish in the past, why should these ones be any different.

Arella gets out of the water not long after Nashoba gets in. Although she is enjoying the feeling of the water on her skin, the weightlessness of floating in it and the feeling of being clean, she has things to do. After making sure none of the men are looking in her direction, Arella climbs out of the clear water and quickly dresses herself. She knows her clothes need washing too, but her spares were left when they ran from the bear. All of their spare clothes were left then. It was the one bag they forgot to pick up in their panic. She pulls on her boots, fixing her dagger in place and begins exploring the place she has chosen as their final camp.

# Chapter 13

The path leads around the back of the waterfall and out towards the other side. Once dressed, Arella picks up her grathon and starts walking. As she passes under the waterfall, she notices more of the strange purple mushrooms growing on the wall. That will be useful. She shouts through to Nootau, her voice echoing off the walls, reaching him clearly. "There are more mushrooms here. Make sure to apply them to Nashoba's chest when he gets out of the water." She does not wait for a response. One is not needed, she simply carries on walking, exploring the way ahead to make sure it is safe.

Arella has always had a good sense of direction, but that is on the ground. The trees and sunlight made it easy to traverse. She knew them like the back of her hand and always assumed that she could find her way around so easily because of this. However, her journey up through the mountains has taught her that she is just naturally good at knowing where to go. Arella is confident that in a short while, she will be able to see the green, and that she will know that they are close to their destination.

There is less snow up here now, and it is getting warmer. The further Arella travels, the warmer it is becoming. For the first time in a couple of weeks, Arella is sweating. She wipes her forehead, the sweat leaving a trail on her sleeve. She pulls her hood back down, letting the light breeze blow across her face. She squints ahead, looking for signs of green, and she is not disappointed. Within only half an hour of leaving her group, Arella can see the green. It looks to be a further hour or so away. The path winds and turns in front of her, but she can clearly see that it leads all the way to the green. It shouldn't be too hard to get there.

The green is such a contrast to the grey, brown and white that they have been used to seeing for the last week. It is bright, beautiful and a little daunting. Arella can clearly see trees growing in the green, and although she cannot see all of it, the place looks to be large. There is a large rock in the middle, an extension of the mountain, and there is a sea of green on either side. Arella can also see the source of the river, falling from a rock in the green down and flowing towards her, soon to be hidden by more rock before coming out at the camp she has chosen in the form of a waterfall.

Arella looks back on herself, towards the group. Now even

though it only took her about half an hour to get to this point, it will take double that time with the others in tow. Arella looks up at the sky and the falling sun. Only about another hour and it will be dark. It's a good job she decided to leave them at the waterfall, and to camp there the night. Granted they would already be at the green by now, but they still do not know what they will find there. For all they know if could be filled with skinwalkers, or nasty beasts like the strange thing in the low forest, or maybe even worse. Arella doesn't want to dwell on these thoughts too much. She will deal with the danger when it comes to it. For now though she must get back to the others and make some food. Her stomach rumbles at the thought of eating fish. It's been a long time since she's eaten fresh fish.

She walks back to the group, finding them all sat around talking. Nashoba is looking better again, his wound not quite as purple, although maybe this is because there is less dirt in it. They all smile as she comes closer, happy to see her. "You were gone a while." Nashoba says, getting up to meet her. He places his arms around her and hugs her. Arella hugs him back, breathing in the scent of his clean skin. "We thought you'd abandoned us and were never coming back."

"I would never do that." Arella says, still locked in Nashoba's embrace, her eyes closed and a smile on her face. He lets go all too soon, and Arella is getting withdrawal symptoms from not being held.

"Oh I almost forgot!" She gushes. In her contentment at being held, Arella almost forgot about the green. "I found it."

"Really?" They all say at once.

"It's about two or three hours that way." She points her finger.

"How did you get back so quick? You weren't gone that long were you?" Nashoba asks.

"Well I practically ran, and I stopped long before I got to the green. I went just far enough to be able to see the path there. We shouldn't have any trouble getting there." She smiles.

"That's amazing!" Nashoba rushes, picking Arella up and swinging her around. He winces in pain as he does this. "Ouch, almost forgot about that." He says.

"How does it feel?" Arella asks.

"Much better with the mushrooms. Nootau thinks the others were starting to turn, which is why I went a little funny on them. I feel much better now though." He's still pale, but there is some colour in his cheeks. Arella brings a hand up to his face, brushing her fingers through his stubbly beard.

"This is growing quite a lot." She laughs.

"Not as much as mine though." Mato boasts. It's true, he has the biggest beard of the three men. Nashoba is just stubble, enough to make him look rough around the edges, Nootau's is a little longer, and Mato almost has a full beard.

"You started the journey with stubble though. So you've cheated technically." Nootau quips back.

Arella is too busy to listen to their childish bickering. Nashoba has kissed her, full on the lips in front of everyone. This is a big moment. His lips feel smooth and soft against hers. A stark contrast to his newly formed beard bushing against her chin. His moustache tickles her nose. When the kiss finishes, Arella sneezes. A small sneeze that you'd expect a kitten to make. It's a cute noise. "I'll get rid of the beard and moustache when we get home." He says, laughing.

"If you're quite finished." Nootau laughs. "I think we have a fire to start and some food to catch."

"And what food do you propose Nootau?" Mato asks, toying with him.

"I think I saw some fish in the river." Nootau winks.

"Good job I'm way ahead of you on that one Nootau." Arella laughs. "You guys go get the fire set up and I'll catch tea. Or do you want to give it another go Mato?" Everyone bursts into laughter at this, remembering the last time Mato tried to catch fish.

"It was hard." He pouts.

"It's okay Mato. Just go make the fire." She laughs again.

Out of the seven fish Arella manages to catch, Maska ends up with three of them. They aren't very big, but one fish each will do then a decent meal. Each fish have bright coloured scales. Some are bright pink with patches of red scales, while others are a deep grey with black. Arella has never seen fish like this before, but then again she has never seen a waterfall river in the mountains before either.

After gutting and slicing strips off the fish, Arella places them over sticks and rests them over the open flames of the fire Mato has made. The whole of the group sit around, cloaks off for the first time outside in a long time. The air here is much warmer than it should be at the top of the mountain, but they all decide it's better not to question it. The spirits work in wonderful ways, and if they've decided that the top of the mountain should be warm, then who are they to question it.

The meat of the fish is sweet and juicy. Some of the best food Arella has eaten in a long long time. She gorges herself on it. They all do. With juicy flesh, flaking away from the crispy skin with every bite, there isn't much conversation. Nootau notices this and in true Nootau fashion, decides to break the silence. "So what's the first thing you're going to do when you get home?" He asks the group, a mouth full of fish muffling his words a little.

"I'm going to eat until I can't move anymore." Mato laughs.

"Don't you do that anyway?" Nashoba shoots at him.

"Don't be mean Nashoba. Mato always has his fair share when he eats with us." Arella smiles.

"You've not seen him eat at home. There's no fair share about it then." Nootau laughs. What about you Arella?"

"I haven't really thought about it." She says, thinking for a second. "I think I'm going to eat grue bulbs and berries, and lots of them, then sleep in my bed, all warm and cosy... Not on the ground. I'm going to change my clothes too. These are getting pretty uncomfortable." She takes a bite of fish. "What about you Nootau? Seen as though you asked, you must have something you want to share."

"I want to get myself a girl." He smiles.

"Whoa man! Too much information there." Mato laughs.

"I don't mean like that, but look at them." He gestures to Nashoba and Arella. "They look lovely together. I want some of that."

"Ooohhhh, someone's jealous." Mato taunts.

"Oh shut up." Nootau goes red. "What about you?" He says to Nashoba, trying to deflect the unwanted attention. "What will you do?"

"I'm going to take back my village and make everything right again." He says in a serious tone. "Then I'm going to eat. A lot." They all laugh at this, but Arella can still see the seriousness in his deep green eyes.

With full bellies and the moos rising into the sky, it seems like everyone is getting ready to sleep. Arella and Nashoba will take first watch, then wake Nootau and Mato for the second. This place is too exposed for them to just sleep without a guard, and they still do not know what might be living this far up the mountain. Arella decides to ask Nashoba about what is going to happen when they get back to the village.

"Honestly, I don't know." He admits. "What I want is for you to come back to the village with me, live we me and for us all to get along."

"But..." Arella pushes.

"But I honestly can't see that happening." He says. "The people in my tribe are set in their ways. They see you as dangerous, and I'm not sure how to change their minds." He looks sad.

"Can I share something with you?" Arella asks, not looking Nashoba in the eye.

"Anything." He says.

"My old tribe, the one I was born into, were very set in their ways. They were killed by a passing raiding party. None of them survived. If your tribe do not change the way they think, the way they see things, they are all going to meet a similar fate. I mean, you had to change the way you see things right?"

"How do you mean?"

"The first time you saw me what did you think? Honestly now Nashoba, I can tell when you're lying."

"I thought you were a ghost. You know that." He says, confused at her questions.

"And what emotion did that bring. What did you feel when you thought you saw a ghost?" She pushes further, hoping he sees where she is going with this.

"I was scared. I'd never seen anyone so pale or beautiful in my life. I didn't know what to think." He says. Arella looks deep into his green eyes, seeing nothing but honesty.

"And do you think I'm scary now?" She asks.

"You're not scary at all." He laughs, then realises what she's just been saying. "Oh… I get it."

"If you were always scared of me, how do you think this would have gone?" She asks. This might be getting dangerous now. She might be pushing things a step too far.

"I don't know." He says. Nashoba has no idea what the pale girl is getting at.

"I'd be dead." She says as if it is the only answer.

"No you wouldn't." He argues.

"I would. If you were always scared of me, I would have been killed at your village when I helped with the raid. If not there, you would have let your sister kill me in the forest, or let the wound the bison caused finish me off."

"I would never have done that." Nashoba says, a little hurt.

"I think you would. Not because you wanted to hurt me, but because I was something to fear. Things that are frightening are better off gone."

"But it was you helping at the raid that changed my mind." Nashoba finishes, annoyed that Arella is not listening to him. Then he realises. That is exactly what she's been trying to say. The only reason she is alive now if because Nashoba changed his mind about her. "Well if I can convince my friends to like you, then why not the rest of the village?" He's talking to himself more than Arella, but she answers anyway.

"You can try." She says. Nashoba's hand takes hold of hers, and he squeezes tight. She squeezes back and smiles at him. They share a kiss under the light of the winter moon.

# Chapter 14

Darkness is all around when Arella opens her eyes. She's fallen asleep. This is not good. She and Nashoba were on guard duty. She looks around for him, checking to see if he is awake or if he too fell asleep. "Don't worry Arella. I stayed awake." His familiar voice sounds from the blackness. "I just got up for a walk to keep me awake. I think it's about time to wake Nootau and Mato for their shift though." Arella sits up, her head still groggy.

"How long was I out?" She asks.

"Not long." He says. "An hour or so maybe?"

Arella allows her eyes to adjust to the darkness, then stands with Nashoba. She looks out over the river. The silver light of the moon reflects on its surface. This reminds her of home. The moon used to do that on the water at home too. She is suddenly feeling quite homesick and sad. Her life has changed so much in such a short space of time. She can only hope things continue to change for her, and for the better.

Nashoba wakes Nootau and Mato so they can take shift. Arella takes herself off into her furs and wraps up warm. She is soon joined by Nashoba, who lays down next to her. Maska is snoring loudly, but this is masked slightly by the sound of the waterfall. The fire they made earlier that night has almost gone out, but the air here is warmer than they are used to of late, and the fire is not needed as much. It doesn't take long for Arella to drop back off to sleep again.

They switch shifts again twice during the night, but nothing happens to have warranted the shift sleeping. Even with the broken night's sleep, Arella wakes feeling refreshed. The morning call of birds is her first indication that it's time to get up. The second is the sun streaming through her eyelids. She sits up with nervous anticipation. This is it. Today is they day they will finally get to the green, finally find out who she really is, and hopefully the mountain spirit will be kind enough to heal Nashoba.

The group pack away their bedding furs and cloaks, no longer needing them in the warmer weather, and set out once again for the green. The heavy bags were left at the waterfall site. It would be too much to carry them to the green, and they did not need the space clothes. The bedding however they would still have to take with them. Mato carried this. He's still the strongest of the group. "It's my daily workout." He's say whenever anyone would ask if he wanted them to take the bedding for a while.

Maska walks on ahead, padding ten feet in front of the rest of the group, smelling all the new smells that line this path. The whole time they have been coming up the mountain, they have been following a path, and a well-worn one at that. "How many people do you think have come this way?" Arella asks.

"I don't know." Nashoba says. "Legends say that not many people who come to the mountains survive. Only the brave and strong, but I haven't heard of anyone coming up here in a long time."

"No one from our tribe has been this far this way." Nootau says. He pauses. "That was badly phrased but you know what I mean."

"Why do you ask?" Mato chimes in from behind.

"Well look at the path." Arella says. The men do so, but seem no wiser.

"It's made of stone. So what?" Nootau laughs.

"It's flat, smooth and there are small weeds growing at the side." She says.

"So no one looks after it." Nootau says.

"Arella what are you getting at here?" Nashoba asks. He knows the pale girl has a tendency to try to make others see what she is trying to tell them without actually saying it.

"The path is looked after." She says finally, giving up on the idea that they might see it for themselves. "The path has been walked a lot, and recently too. I think people really do live up here."

"Well that's a good thing right?" Nootau asks.

"I hope so." Arella says, although she has a funny feeling about this.

"Let's hope one of the people that live up here is a master healer." Nashoba laughs, although it is an empty laugh.

The group round the corner Arella came to the night before, and are instantly met with the beauty of the green that is in front of them. It looks even more beautiful today, looking at it with the sun shining brightly. They all stop and stare at the beauty before them. A paradise of green in the harshness of the snow and rock that surrounds them. "Oh wow." Nootau gasps. "The green is real then."

"Mr state the obvious." Arella says. She's seen this sight before, but it wasn't nearly as beautiful in the dark as it is now in the bright sunlight. "Should we keep going then?"

"No I think we should turn back around and go back to the village." Nootau says sarcastically. "Of course we're going to keep going till we get there."

"Well let's go then." Mato says excitedly.

Arella looks back at Nashoba. He looks pale. Very pale. *"We'd better get there soon."* She frowns. Nashoba doesn't look like he's going to last much longer like this. The spear through his chest is clearly becoming more of a problem, and the wound is sure to be infected by now. Nootau's done a wonderful job with the mushrooms, but with the spear still in his chest, the wound can not heal properly. Once again Arella hopes with all her heart that there is a healer in the green. The men said that the mountain spirit lived up here. Perhaps he is a man, and perhaps there is a tribe up here. Arella hopes they are accepting, and willing to help. She moves next to Nashoba and puts an arm around him, helping him to walk. This time he doesn't push her away or fight against the help.

The green is so close, but still so far away. The more they walk, the further away it seems to be. It is hard walking with Nashoba leaning on her, but Arella keeps going. They have to get to the green, and they have to do it fast. Even if there aren't people up here, there will be plants that can help to save Nashoba, and Nootau will be able to find the resources to save his life.

Nashoba trips on a loose stone, dragging Arella down with him. She hits the ground hard, taking most of the impact. Mato and Nootau rush to the two on the ground, helping them both up. "I'll take him from here." Mato says to Arella.

"I'm okay." She argues but Nootau cuts her off.

"Arella you're knees..." He doesn't need to say anymore than that. She looks down at her blood soaked trousers. When her knees made contact with the ground they caused grazes that are bleeding.

"It probably looks worse than it is." She insists.

"Arella stop. You're going to really hurt yourself if you carry on like this." Mato say, taking Nashoba from under the arm and holding him strong. "You need to be well when we get to the green. It is you who needs to see the mountain spirit, not us." There is no point in Arella arguing. She knows she will lose against the men now. She takes lead of the group again. Maska is still at the head of the group, walking a little way ahead. She can't help but look back at the men behind her, but regrets it every time. They look so tired, so worn out. She really hopes this will be worth it.

The sky begins to grey, and clouds now cover the sun and bright blue that was just an hour before. The temperature in the air drops, and the wind is picking up again. The mountain on the left hand side of the travellers is lowering, and the wind howling over the top is getting closer. With the large drop on the otherside, Arella is a little worried about what will happen when the reach the point that the ground they are walking on is level with the top. She can see it ahead. Luckily, the path seems to widen before that point, and Arella does not plan on walking close to the edge at that point. Looking over the edge, Arella can see clouds beneath her. She can't see the ground, and a little dizziness takes her over. She looks away from the abyss below. Not being able to see the ground makes her feel funny and she decides its probably not the best idea to look at it. Maska however is not bothered by the height. He will happily stand close to the edge and look over. He likes the feeling on being on top of the world, relishes the feeling of the wind in his fur. He's coming alive the more they travel.

The green is coming closer, and the ground has now levelled out. The wind would not have been much of a problem if the group was still strong, but all the walking they have done has made them tired. They are all injured in some kind of way, although Nashoba and Arella have the most of it, Nootau and Mato are also suffering from various cute, bruises and pulled muscles.

Focusing her attention on the gates ahead, Arella picks out the detail. The gates look to be wooden, although they are the bright purple wood her bow is made of. She has a pang of pain as she thinks of that bow, broken but still on her back. The gates are elaborate, wood intertwined and swirled. She wonders to herself how they train the wood to grow like that. It could not have been carved. That kind of work would have taken whoever did it hours. The gates look to be tall, over double her height, and they are surrounded by rocks even higher on either side. The green in enclosed in a stone wall. Arella had not seen this wall before, looking at it as though it were just part of the mountain. "Wait a second...Gates?" She says, suddenly realising what it is she has seen.

"What was that?" Nootau strains, the weight of Nashoba getting too much for him. He hands the weakened warrior to Mato. "Did you say gates?"

"Yeah, look." Arella points to the gates.

"Well I'll be." Nootau says coming up next to the white ghost. "We made it."

"Gates mean people Nootau." Arella says, suddenly now filled with nerves. "What if they don't let us in?"

"They will let us in Arella." Nootau reassures her. "They have to. We've come all this way."


"Hello?!" Arella shouts through the wooden bars of the gates. They're locked, although she cannot see what by. It doesn't look like there is anything holding the gates together, but they will not open. Arella has tried, Nootau had a go, and even Mato, but the gates would not open. "Hello!" Arella shouts again.

"Can we break the wood?" Nootau asks. "It's only wood, shouldn't be hard to break."

"Nootau I wouldn't" Arella warns. She doesn't know why, but she feels that attempting to break the gates would be a bad idea. Nootau takes a large rock from the ground and smashes it against one of the smaller bars on the gate. A bright purple light flashes from the contact point, and Nootau is thrown backwards.

"What the bloody hell was that?" Nootau says from the ground.

"Ancient protection magic." A voice says. "To stop invaders entering our home."

"Who said that?" Arella questions, hearing the voice but unable to pinpoint it. She looks around desperate for the person who owns the strange voice.

"Who is asking?" The voice laughs, still not revealing itself.

"My name is Arella." She says. "We have come for the help of the mountain spirit." She explains. The strange voice breaks into laughter.

"And why would the mountain spirit help you child?" The voice is deep and threatening. Arella doesn't like it, but she has nothing to lose from talking to it. Perhaps this is the mountain spirit and it is testing her.

"We need the help of the spirit. My friend is badly hurt, and without the spirits help I'm afraid he'll die."

"You lie!" The spirit shouts.

"No, it's the truth." Arella persists. "He'll die without medical help, and soon."

"This is true." The voice agrees. "But this is not the reason you came here. Tell me the truth girl."

"We came for answers. But I no longer need them. All I want now is to save my friend." Arella insists. The voice appears at the gate, the person now revealing himself. The man behind the gate is cloaked in black, no human features visible. Arella can see dark hair under the hood of the cloak, but nothing more of this person. He's tall though, over a head taller than Arella, maybe even taller than Mato, but not as well built from the look of him. The cloak he wears is made from black fur, although Arella does not know what kind of animal the fur comes from. "Please, you have to let us in." Arella begs.

"The glade does not accept outsiders." The stranger says. "You have wasted your time."

"Listen here you!" Nootau shouts at the stranger, pointing his angry finger at him. "You let us in now or I'll..."

"You'll what boy?" The stranger laughs. "The gate is between us. You cannot harm me. You're empty threats are not making me want to let you in."

"Right!" Nootau storms back towards the gate. Arella steps in front of him.

"Nootau stop. This is hopeless. You're not going to get through the gate." Nootau's shoulders drop and he looks down at the ground.

"I know." He says, defeated.

"Please?" Arella turns back around to the stranger at the gate. "We need you're help."

"No. You need to leave." The stranger says.

Arella looks over at Nashoba. His skin is turning blue, and his eyes are almost closed. Mato is now holding his whole weight. He looks worried, and for good reason. Nashoba looks as though he's going to collapse at any moment. Just as Arella turns to look back at the stranger, pleading for help one last time, Nashoba drops to the ground. His body starts to convulse, and twists in strange directions. He's shaking all over. She rushes to his side, kneeling on the ground next to him. His body continues to shake. "It's okay Nashoba, we're here." She says with a thick throat. She's only seen this happen to someone a couple of times, and neither of those people survived the convulsions. She turns to look back at the stranger, her eyes pleading with him, tears welling up in her eyes, the purple shining brighter. The stranger turns away from them, walking away, leaving Nashoba to die outside the gates of the only place that could have saved him.

Nashoba's convulsions finally stop, and his body goes still. Arella is panicking. Her breathing has gone ragged, and she's feeling dizzy and light headed. She looks down at her friend's body on the floor. He's not moving. Why is he not moving? Nootau puts two fingers to Nashoba's neck. Arella stares intently at him. Nootau turns to look at Arella, his fawn brown eyes wet with tears. He opens his mouth to speak, but no sound comes out. "No, no, no." Arella says. "No. He can't be. No!" She shouts. The tears in her eyes fall to the ground, joined by the rain from the sky.

Nootau is still on the ground next to Nashoba's lifeless body. He has his head in his hands, the braids in his hair coming loose. The feathers fell from his hair long ago. Only one remains. Nootau's shoulders shake a little but he makes no noise. Everything is moving in slow motion. Arella can't quite believe that this has happened. Nashoba just can't be dead. He can't be. They've come this far. She looks over at Mato, still standing. There is no emotion on his face. He's just staring at the lifeless body of his friend. Not moving, not speaking, not a tear in his eyes. Just staring. Arella follows his gaze to Nashoba on the ground. His eyes are closed, and his long hair covers most of his face, now matted with the blood that came from his mouth.

Arella's sadness is quickly overtaken by guilt. "This is all my fault." She says, her voice barely audible. "This is my fault." She says, this time louder. Nootau looks up at her, his eyes wet with tears.

"Don't say that." He says to her.

"It is." She says again. The tears in her eyes dry now, replaced by anger. "If I hadn't brought you up here, he wouldn't have died." She's angry at herself.

"Arella listen." Nootau says, controlling his own tears. "This is not your fault." Nootau stands, taking hold of Arella, holding her arms steady.

"Yes it is!" She shouts pulling away from him.

"No, no it isn't." Nootau insists.

"How? How can you say it's not my fault?"

"It was Nashoba who suggested the mountain spirit." He says. "It was his idea."

"But I should have said no." Arella says. The tears fill her eyes again, turning the purple in her eyes a brighter purple. "It's all my fault and now he's dead." The tears are falling again now. Nootau takes her in his arms, holding her tight as she cried. "I loved him, and now he's gone."

Arella is aware of Nootau holding her, but she just feels cold, and it's not the icy rain biting at her skin, soaking into her clothes, but loneliness. Mato soon joins them, putting his large arms around both of them, but still the cold does not subside.

Arella stops her tears. *"I will not cry anymore. This is my fault, and I can't feel sorry for myself. I have to be strong for the others. Oh god, what will we tell Nashoba's tribe? They will not accept me now, and they will be chief-less. Maybe Mato or Nootau will take over. Will the tribe let them back in now that Nashoba is dead?"* These thought now fill Arella's mind. She pulls away from Nootau and Mato.

"We have to take his body back." She says, now much calmer, focused.

"Why? We should bury him here." Mato says. "It's peaceful by the waterfall. He could rest there."

"No we have to take him back. Your tribe have to see that it was skinwalkers who killed him, and not you or I." Arella explains. "If they think either of us killed him they won't let you back in the tribe."

"Oh." Mato says.

Arella's concentration is suddenly broken by a loud roaring sound. She turns back towards the way they came and sees the creature that made the sound. It's the bear, the one that attacked them in the cave just after Nashoba was struck with the spear. "Crap!" She shouts, picking her grathon up from the ground where it lays. The others are too emotional to have noticed the threat the bear causes, or maybe they just don't care anymore, but Arella is just angry. She's going to use this anger to kill the bear. It might make her feel better, or the bear might kill her, even better. If the beast kills her, she won't have to feel the pain of his death anymore. She lifts the grathon up and looks directly at the bear, walking forwards to meet it.

The rain is pouring down, making the ground underfoot rather slippery. Arella moved forwards, and so does the bear. She is now only thirty feet away from it. The bear rears up on its hind legs, roaring at the white girl who stands in front of him, challenging her. "Bring it on bear!" Arella shouts at the beast. A bright strike of lightening fills the sky, followed by a clap of thunder. "You've tracked me this far, why don't you finish me off!" Arella shouts, letting her anger out. Behind her, Nootau and Mato are still by Nashoba's body. "Arella!" Nootau shouts to her.

"Not now Nashoba!" She shouts back to him without turning around. She keeps her eyes focused on the bear. "This bear and me have business." She says more quietly, her eyes not leaving the red beast in front of her.

The bear roars again, saliva flying from its mouth, mingling with the falling rain. It shown all its teeth, bright white and sharp, threatening Arella, goading her to attack it. Arella takes this and runs for the bear with all her speed. She tilts the grathon forwards, one of the spear ends pointing towards the bear, and charges, screaming her battle-cry as she goes. The bear drops to all fours and runs towards her.

Behind this, behind the gates into the glade, the stranger in black is back. He's watching through the gates, watching the scene unfold in front of him.

Arella and the bear come together, but she is not strong enough for it. The beast moves to the side quickly, catching Arella's side, and shoving her over. It continues on, charging towards Nootau, Mato and Nashoba's body. From her place on the ground, now covered in mud and soaked, Arella turns to see the bear charging right for her friends. Anger fills her again and she gets to her feet quickly. Once she has regained her footing, she chases after the bear. It is now that she sees the man in black behind the gate. More anger fills her. He's not going to do anything. He's not going to help.

The bear is upon the men before Arella can get to them, but it is not trying to kill Nootau or Mato. Arella looks around as she runs, searching for Maska. Just as she is wondering where he is, he appears. The great black auron cat, hidden by the dark of the rocks and the darkened sky leaps from behind a rock and dives onto the back of the bear, biting and clawing at it. The bear roars in pain, rearing up in an attempt to rid itself of the pest on its back.

Arella reaches her friends finally. Another flash of lightening and crack of thunder fill the sky, then another. They're getting closer together, and the rain falling harder. Maska leaps from the bears back and moves next to Arella, putting himself between the four of them and the bear. Arella is breathing hard, and steam escapes her mouth. Her warm breath mixing with the cold air.

The red beast calms itself and turns to Arella and the men. It bears its white teeth and roars loud, then looks down at Nashoba's lifeless body. Arella follows its gaze, keeping her grathon raised to it. She looks closely at him. There is something strange about his body. She focuses her eyes, difficult in the rain. Then she notices. There is a small cloud in front of his mouth, and his chest is raising and falling slightly. He's not dead. The others have noticed this too. "Is he breathing?" Nootau says. He's not really questioning it. He can see that Nashoba is breathing, but how is that possible?

A bright purple light fills the sky, causing the group to all look towards it. It is coming from where the bear was standing. Arella shields her eyes from the blinding light with her hand. When the light subsides, the bear is no longer there. In its place stands a man wearing a red bearskin. The man raises his head, revealing his pale white skin beneath. Arella can't quite believe what she is seeing. This man has the same coloured skin as her. Maybe she is not alone in this world.

The man's white skin is perfect. It looks as though there is not a single blemish on it. His top half is naked aside from the bear fur on his back His chiselled chest looks like it could have been carved from stone, and looks hard enough to have been too. The man has strong features on his face. A strong jaw line hidden beneath a blonde beard. The man's hair can be seen from beneath the head of the bear, long and white, braided many times and tied off with leather ribbons. It comes just below his shoulders. The man looks up, locking eyes with Arella. She inhales deeply when she notices the colour of his eyes. Purple. The same bright purple as hers.

# Chapter 15

The white man in the bear skin steps forwards, moving towards Nashoba. "Stop right there!" Arella says, holding her grathon up to the white man. She steps forwards, making sure she is directly in front of Nashoba, blocking him from view of the bear-man. Maska moves too, putting himself in front of Arella. He's protecting her too. "Don't take another step skinwalker."

"I mean you no harm." The white man says. His voice sounds like music, and there is something familiar about it. Arella ignores this.

"You mean us no harm?" She asks sarcastically. "Which is why you tried to kill us in the cave then followed us all the way up here right?" She glances down at Nashoba. His eyes flutter open at the sound of her voice. The green in them is dull, but he is alive. He opens his mouth to speak, but no sound comes out. Nootau moves to him, kneeling by his side, helping him sit up.

"Slowly Nashoba." He whispers to him.

"I wasn't trying to kill you in the cave. I was going to help you." The bear-man explains.

"And why should we believe that?" Arella asks. She is suspicious of this man.

"I give you my word." He says.

"The word of a skinwalker means nothing." Arella spits at him.

"Not all skinwalkers are the same." The bear-man tries.

"The only skinwalkers I have ever spoken to have tried to kill me, why would you be any different?" She asks.

"Because if you don't trust me, your friend there is going to die." He says matter-o-factly. Arella knows this is true. Nashoba is in bad shape, and this man might be her only help. "I can get you into the glade, and I can ask the healer to look at your friend." He insists. "But you have to trust me"

Arella looks at Nashoba. Nootau has got him standing, but he looks extremely weak. She pleads with him for an answer, but the look in his eyes say it all. "Okay." Arella says, not even looking at the bear-man. "I will trust you." She turns to look at him. "But if Nashoba dies, so do you." She points the grathon at the white man. "Do you understand?"

"Completely." The man says. He steps forwards, moving around the group. They're weary of this man, but if he can help Nashoba get better, what do they have to lose. The chances are they would die on the way back to the village without the healer in the glade.

"Open the gate Elsu." The white man says.

"I don't think that's a good idea Kuruk." The black cloaked man says. He steps up to the gate, revealing his face in the lightening. He too has white skin, but his face is not so appealing. He has a slight hooked nose.

"Elsu as your chief I am telling you to open the gate now." The white man called Kuruk commands.

"You need to learn to leave well enough alone 'chief'." The black cloaked man says.

"What's going on here?" Another voice says. Arella can see the man walking towards the gate. He is wearing what looks to be a brown feathered cloak.

"Elsu has decided that we are no longer letting other skinwalkers into the glade Migisi." Kuruk says.

"Other skinwalkers?" Migisi says. He has dark brown skin, the same as the men she travelled to the mountains with. His hair is cut short to his head, and he has a tattoo of a feather on his left cheek. "Oh the young skinwalker and her friends." The gates open with a click and a flash of purple light. The swing open slowly, and the glade inside can be seen clearly. It looks beautiful, but at the moment it is the last thought on Arella's mind.

"I'm not a skinwalker." She says.

"Oh but you are my dear." Migisi says as he steps forwards. Elsu has gone quiet, retreating into the depths of the glade. Arella doesn't even see him go. "You don't recognise me do you child?" He asks Arella.

"No, who are you?" She's puzzled by him. Migis steps backwards, looks up into the sky and breathes in deep. He closes his eyes, and which a flash of purple, he transforms. The thing that replaces the man that stood before her is a great brown eagle. The same eagle that helped save her and the men from the flock of crows just a couple of days before. None of them can quite believe their eyes.

"Okay, I get that this is amazing and all, but we need to get Nashoba seen to now." Nootau pipes up.

"Of course." Kuruk says. "Migisi, please turn back and help me with the boy." The eagle before them transforms into the man again and he and the bear-man step forwards, taking the tired and pale looking Nashoba from Nootau and Mato. They lead him through the gate.

Arella is still suspicious of these people. She plans on keeping a very close eye on them.

Kuruk leads them to a cave in the side of the mountain. When they enter, Arella is instantly met with a beautiful scent. It smells like freshly cut flowers. The cave is bright inside, lit by several small fires burning in different places. Above some of these fires there is meat cooking. It smells divine. There is only one person in this cave other than those who just entered. A thin old woman is sitting by a stone slab at the back of the cave. She stands when Nashoba is brought in, moving over to inspect him.

"Is this the boy you were telling me about Migisi?" The old woman rasps. "He looks worse than you explained."

"He's gotten worse since I saw him." Migisi explains. He and Kuruk guide Nashoba to the stone slab. They help him onto it, then lie him backwards. Arella enters further into the cave and stands next to Nashoba.

"Is he going to be okay?" She asks.

"Let me look at him child." The old woman says. "I'm going to give him something to help him sleep. That way I can work on him better." The woman begins digging around in her dried plants, moving them aside, picking them up and putting them back down again, deciding what she should use.

"Can I watch?" Nootau asks, a little shy. He's not normally shy, but these people intimidate him. "I want to be a healer." He pushes.

"It won't be pretty boy." The old woman says, a small smile on her pretty wrinkled face. "But you can stay if you want."

"I would like to stay too." Arella says, holding Nashoba's hand tight. The wolf around her neck burns hot.

"Me too." Mato says. "We're all staying with him until he's better."

"Don't you trust me?" The old woman asks. Arella looks deep

into her dark eyes. She can trust this woman. There is no malice behind her eyes, no intention to do wrong by them. Nashoba is in good hands here.

The old woman finds what she is looking for, a purple plant with bright yellow pollen. She puts it in a mortar and begins grinding it up. "This is a special flower that only grows here in the glade." She explains as Nootau looks on questioningly.

"What is it called?" He asks.

"It does not have a name." The old woman explains. "We do not need a name for it here."

"Tuwa, do you need anything?" Migisi asks.

"No child. You can do if you like. You too Kuruk. The children will still be here in the morning." With that the two men leave the cave.

"Just shout if you need anything." Kuruk says. "We will not be far away."

The woman goes back to Nashoba. She takes the mortar with the ground up flowers in it, and places it next to Nashoba on the stone slab. "You will need to hold him down for this." Tuwa says. Nootau and Mato each take a side, and Arella stands at Nashoba's head. She places her hands on his shoulders and holds him steady. Arella bends and kisses him on the forehead.

"We're all right here Nashoba." She says to him. He's fallen unconscious again, but he is still breathing at least.

Tuwa takes some of the flowers from the mortar and opens Nashoba's mouth. She places the purple paste in his mouth. Nashoba instantly begins to shake. Arella and the men hold him down. "Is this meant to happen?" Nootau asks. Maska has now moved inside the cave and is standing watch close by. He's not entirely sure he trusts the people here either, but he has no proof to say that there is anything untoward about them. He will simply keep watch until they leave the glade and go back home.

The shaking stops after about a minute, and Nashoba relaxes again. "What did that do?" Arella asks.

"Calms him, takes away any pain he might be feeling, or might be about to feel." Tuwa says. "What I am about to do to him will be extremely painful. The spear has been inside his chest for a long time, and the skin around it has begun healing to the wood." Arella looks closely at the wound in Nashoba's chest. The old woman is right. She looks at Tuwa's wrinkled pale hands. They are steady, very steady for someone who is so old. She takes a sharp dagger from beside her and brings it to Nashoba's chest. "I must cut the skin attached to the spear before I can pull it out." She explains. "This will cause some blood, and it would cause him a lot of pain if I had not given him the flowers." She then uses the dagger to cut the swollen infected skin from the spear.

A feeling of dizziness comes over Arella. She turns more pale than normal, and a hot sick feeling rises in her throat. *"Hold it together girl."* She says to herself. *"You have to be here for him the whole way through."* She steadies herself, takes a deep breath, and continues watching.

The old woman places the now blood stained dagger on the slab of stone. Her pale wrinkled hands are no longer white, but are now red with Nashoba's blood. She takes hold of the spear and gives it a pull. It comes away from Nashoba's chest, and the cavity is instantly filled with deep red blood. "Cloth now." The old woman says. Nootau rushes quickly, taking the cloths from the side and handing them to the woman. She pushes the absorbent cloth against the wound. "You need to hold this down, and hold it firm." Tuwa says to Arella. She does just this, putting pressure on the wound with the cloth to stem the bleeding.

"Where are you going?" Arella asks as Tuwa moves away from Nashoba.

"I need to get a bonding agent. I did not realise the wound would be so vast." Tuwa admits. She rushes to the other side of the cave, rummaging around in the piles of things that line the walls. She finally comes back, bringing with her what looks like honey.

"What's that?" Arella asks. She's beginning to panic again now.

She can feel the cloth becoming hot and wet beneath her hands. The blood is seeping through.

"It's honey, but not just any honey. This is honey from the Tubba bee. They only live here in the glade, and their honey has healing properties and is an amazing bonding agent." Tuwa explains.

"No offence lady." Mato says. "But could you please hurry up and save our friend?"

"Of course child." Tuwa says. The old woman tucks her grey hair behind her ears and comes next to Nashoba again. "Okay girl, take the cloths away and have your hands ready. I'm going to fill the wound with the honey, and I need you to push the skin together." Arella looks worried.

"I don't know if I can..."

"Arella you have to." Nootau pleads. Arella summons all her strength and nods.

"Okay."

Tuwa gives the signal, and Arella pulls the cloths away from Nashoba's chest. She drops them on the slab and readies her hands. The old woman fills the hold in Nashoba's chest with the honey, then looks at Arella. She places her shaking hands on either side of the wound and presses them together as hard as she can. The wound slowly comes together, and soon there is not flesh to e seen beneath the skin on Nashoba's bare chest. Once the wound is together, Tuwa takes a sharp boroana spine and some thread and begins threading the wound back together. This does not take long, and soon the bleeding has stopped. Once the stitching is done, Tuwa takes more clean cloth and places it on the wound, securing it in place by wrapping it around Nashoba's chest.

Nashoba's eyes flutter open a little, then pain fills his face. He cries out, and Tuwa is quick to bring the purple flowers back. "You must sleep until you are healed." She says over his cries, putting the flowers to his mouth and forcing him to eat them. He calms almost instantly, no shaking this time.

"How long will it be until he is better again?" Arella asks, holding his hand tight in hers.

"The honey should heal him quickly, but I have no way of telling." Tuwa says.

"Thank you." Arella says to the old woman.

"Don't thank me child. It's the least I could do. There is food on the fire, and you can sleep here in my cave tonight." She says as she exits the cave.

Arella follows Tuwa to the cave entrance. When she is sure they are alone, she walks back to the others at Nashoba's bedside. "Are you guys sure we can trust them?" She asks.

"Well they helped us with Nashoba, and he's alive." Nootau says.

"I guess. But something about them is strange." Arella continues.

"I think you're over reacting." Mato says, already tucking into some of the meat cooking over the flames. "They seem fine to me, and this meat is amazing."

"What is it?" Arella and Nootau ask, mouths watering at the smell of the food.

"Tastes like deer to me." Mato says. He takes another bite, hot juices dripping down his beard. "Yep, definitely deer." The others take meat from the fire too and begin eating.

Arella has returned to Nashoba's side. She sits with one hand on his, and the other taking the meat to and from her mouth as she eats. "We made it Nashoba." She says to the unconscious man. "We're here, at the green, the glade, whatever they call it. As soon as you're better, we'll go back to your village. When we tell them of what you've been through, and the dangers you've faced, they're sure to accept you back as the chief."

"Of course they will." Nootau smiles. "Nashoba is chief by birth, and he has earned his title."

"I think he'll be the youngest chief in over 100 years you know." Mato says, his mouth full of food. "And no doubt the best."

"He will be the best, because he has you guys too." Arella smiles.

"And you." Nootau nods towards the white ghost. "Do you still have that wolf necklace he gave you?" Arella's hand reaches for the stone wolf and pulls it out from under her shirt.

"I will never let it go." She smiles down at Nashoba.


Once they have had their fill of food, being careful to leave some meat for when Nashoba wakes up, Nootau begins tending to their remaining wounds. Most of them are superficial, and the only wound that needs proper attention is the cut to Arella's knee. Once cleaned up and bandaged, it is not more than a small scratch. "They always look worse than they are." Nootau says.

"I think you're getting good at this healer thing." Arella laughs.

"Yeah." Mato agrees. "I only wish he was this good when we came across that bear on our trial." He points at the scar covering one side of his face. He then breaks out into laughter.

"I don't know Mato, I think it suits you." Nootau quips back.

"Should we give you one too? It might suit you more." Mato says back to him.

"I've missed this." Arella says.

"Missed what?" Nashoba croaks. They all turn to look at him. He's awake. Tired and groggy looking, but awake. Arella throws her arms around him. Nashoba groans in pain at the force of her hug. She tries to pull away, regretting grabbing him so hard, but he holds her close. "I'm not letting you go anywhere." He whispers.

With a little effort, they manage to get Nashoba sitting up. Arella can tell he's in some pain, but already the wound on his chest is looking better. The reddish purple from around the wound is going down, and it doesn't look as swollen as it did before. "So remind me what has happened for the last few days?" Nashoba asks as he chews deer.

"How much do you remember?" Arella asks.

"Not much. I remember us being in a cave, and I think I remember crows. The next thing I remember is being here."

"You really don't remember much do you?" Nootau says.

"Not really no." Nashoba says again, a mouth full of food. "Where are we even?"

"We found the green, but the people who live here call it the glade." Arella explains. "We've met four people so far. There's Kuruk; he seems to be the chief, Migisi, he's the eagle who saved us from the crows..."

"The what?" Nashoba starts to panic. "These are skinwalkers?"

"Yeah, but I think they're okay." Arella tries.

"We were nearly killed... I was nearly killed by skinwalkers. How can these ones be any different?"

"They saved you." Arella says.

"One of them is funny though." Nootau says.

"I agree. The one in the black was funny looking, and he was all up for leaving us outside the gates. Elsu? Was that his name?" Mato agrees.

"I guess so, but then there's Tuwa too." Arella finishes.

"Who's Tuwa?" Nashoba asks.

"The old lady. She's the one who healed you." Nootau answers.

"Do we really have any reason to not trust these people?" Arella asks. She's now doubting her own negative thoughts of these people. "They took us in, fed us and healed us. They can't be all bad, skinwalkers I mean."

"I still don't trust them." Nashoba says. "I'm grateful for their help, but I want to get out of here as soon as we have the answer to your question Arella." He says, turning to look at her. "Tomorrow we ask them where to find the mountain spirit, and you get your answers."

"I don't need answers anymore Nashoba." Arella smiles. "I know who I am. I'm Arella. I'm the White Ghost. I'm me. I don't need anyone to tell me that. I know who I am."

"Good." The men all say in unison. Maska purrs softly at Arella's side.

"I have my friends, my family, and I don't care what people think of me anymore." She smiles again, this time bigger than she has ever smiled before.

# Chapter 16

Once again, everyone is asleep, but dreams are evading Arella. Lying in the cave, staring at the stone roof, waiting for the dreams to take her. Nashoba, Nootau, Mato and Maska are all snoring. This noise has become comforting, loud, but familiar. The fact that they are snoring means they are all comfortable, safe and more importantly, happy. Arella smiles and closes her eyes, listening to the sounds the glade is creating. She can hear an owl, hooting somewhere in a tree, the slow pitter patter of rain falling on the soft green grass outside, the chirping of crickets in the dark.

"What about the girl?" Arella hears whispered voices outside. She opens her eyes, orange peeking over the horizon, just starting to light the sky up. Arella knows she must have fallen asleep.

"What about her, she's no concern of ours." Another whispered voice says.

"She is." The first voice says again.

"Kuruk, I know you asked me to save them from our crows, but why?" The second voice asks.

"We put those protections up for ourselves Migisi. The crows were meant to protect us from dangers. But those children are not dangerous." Kuruk explains. Arella strains her ears to listen harder. This could be interesting, and these people are talking about her and her friends.

"What if they are dangerous?" Migisi asks. "I mean, would the crows have attacked them if they weren't a danger to us?"

"I believe so yes. I've not really seen them in action. We've never really used them before." Kuruk explains.

"Remind me why we put these protections on the glade anyway. It's been years since I've heard this one, and I can barely remember the details anymore."

"Do you remember when Enyeto and Myla left the village, taking the others with them?" Kuruk starts.

"I remember yeah, we lost half our village that year."

"Well we put the protections up then. That same year, Elsu's brother left too. Do you remember him?"

"He was strange. What was his name again? I never really spoke to him."

"Wattan. That was his name." Kuruk continues.

"Wasn't he the same black bird his brother turns into?" Migisi asks.

"Yes he was, although he went too far with his transformations. It turned him mad. Eventually, he could not turn back into his human form, and was instead stuck somewhere in-between. When he left, as well as Enyeto and the others, ~I decided we should protect ourselves. Skinwalker magic is powerful, and who knows what would happen if it were to fall into the wrong hands.

Some skinwalkers can even control animals you know?"

"Is that what you think the girl does with that auron cat?"

"No, I think the beast follows her of his own volition, but she is a skinwalker for sure. I know that just from looking at her." Kuruk says.

"How would you know that?" Migisi questions.

"Because she's my daughter."

Arella can't quite believe what she just heard. Did he just say that she was his daughter. How can that be? For starters Nayleen had told her raft her father was an invader from another tribe and that he raped her mother. If this man is her father, that would mean that he raped her mother. Even though Arella doesn't remember the wam who brought her into this world, the thought that someone could hurt her is still real.

Arella can see resemblances between her and the people of this tribe. They all have the se coloured skin, but that is as far as it goes in her eyes. Another thing is that these people are skinwalkers and she is not. She is not able nod never has been able to turn into an animal and cannot see the benefit in being able to. She decides to listen more. Maybe she will get some answers or at least be able to disprove Kuruk.

"What do you mean she's your daughter? You have no children."
Migisi says.

"It was about nineteen years ago." Kuruk begins. "I travelled away
from the glad in search of more seeds to bring back here. We'd been
hot bad by the winter and a lot of the seeds of gathered from the
years before has not taken root."

"I travelled quote a way, past the forest at the foot of the
mountain, through the red waste where nothing grows and through
another forest. I found plenty of new fruit there but I also found
something else. There was a young lady, young twenties and
beautiful. She had long dark hair and the deepest of eyes. I watched
her for a while. She was by a small stream, cleaning her clothes. She
really was the most beautiful thing I had ever seen. Her skin was a
delicious dark caramel colour, and I couldn't stop watching her. No
matter how hard I tried I could not pull my eyes away from this
beautiful woman." Arella hears Kuruk say.

"So what happened next?" Migisi asks, wanting to know as much as
Arella does.

"After watching for a while I approached her. I expected her to be
frightened of me, but she wasn't. She was more intrigued by my
pale skin and hair than anything else."

"We spoke for a long while. She asked me where I came from, who I was and why I was so far from home. I told her everything and she listened she believed. It had been so long since I'd spoken with someone from outside our tribe who was not afraid of us. I asked her about herself and what her tribe was like. She told me everything too."

"After a few days of meeting up with the young woman in secret, she wanted me to meet with her father. She wanted to show me off to him, get his approval. Is fallen head over heels with this girl and I agreed to meet her father."

"And how did that go? Migisi asks. Arella thinks she has an idea already of how that meeting might have gone.

"We'll I met with her father. She took me right into her village. There was one thing she neglected to tell me..."

"Don't leave me in suspense Kuruk, what is it?" Migisi echoes Arella's thoughts.

"Her father was the chief." Kuruk says.

Arella can't believe what she's hearing. He must have the wrong girl. Her mother was not daughter of the chief. Her mother was just some girl who died bringing her into this world.

"Chief? Wow bet that was a shock."

"Just a bit." Kuruk laughs. "Safe to say I did not get his blessing. His daughter was already in love with me though. We were going to run away together."

"What happened?" Migisi asks.

"I hung around for a few more weeks, but the chief was becoming protective. He wouldn't let her out of his site. One day, she just stopped coming to boost me."

"I left and came back to the glade once I had not seen her for over a week. It left me heart broken."

"How do you know the girl is even yours then?" Migisi questions.

"She has her mothers smile." Kuruk says. Arella can tell by the tone of his voice he is smiling. "Do you want to know the sad part?"

"I have a feeling you're going to tell me anyway."

"Once her father discovered she was pregnant, he disowned her. He let her live in the village still, but no longer called him his daughter. Her brother later took over the tribe. I believe this is the only reason the child is still here. Because the girl I fell in love with happened to be the chiefs daughter. Otherwise they would have left her pit to die when her mother died."

"Her mother died? How?" Migisi asks.

"Childbirth I believe. But my before naming the child Arella. It was the name we'd both agreed on."

"So what are you going to do? Will you tell her?"

"I don't know yet. I don't see what either if us could gain from it."

Kuruk says.

"She could be a skinwalkers too. That would be valuable. And she would need to learn to control it." Migisi says.

"Or she could just as easily not be a skinwalker at all. We'll see what the morning brings."

The voices fade off into the distance, and Arella is left with mixed emotions. On the one hand she knows who her father is, and if the story is true, he loved her mother and Arella was born out of love not rape, but on the other hand... She could be a skinwalker.

Even if the sun was not already on its way up, there is no way Arella would be able to go back to sleep. She is wide awake and wants to get up. More than anything now she wants to be away from this place. The fact that she now knows who her father is changes nothing. She wants to get Nashoba back to his village so he can take his rightful place as chief. Arella belongs back down there, in her forest, with her friends around her. Even if she is related to the skinwalker, they are not her family. She wants to leave and forget this place, forget the people that live here and go home. One thing is stopping her from waking the others op now and leaving... Nashoba is not strong enough to travel back yet. He needs another day of resting. Arella has already decided that she will spend the day preparing. She needs to mend her bow, then at least she will be ready to go home.

Arella waits a couple more minutes before getting up from her bed on the ground. She decides not to wake the others yet. Instead she is going to ask Tuwa about the brother of the crow feathered man. He sounds very similar to the description Nashoba have of the thing that killed his father, and Arella wants to know of it is the same creature.

It doesn't take much to find Tuwa. The bright sunlight is almost blinding when Arella leaves the cave, but her eyes soon adjust. She spots Tuwa sitting by a small pond sat under a willow tree. It reminds her a little of the cherry tree she used to sit at when she was thinking of how her life could be. How much her life has changed since then. If someone had told Arella what she would have been through in the next years after she made the decision to leave her village, she would have told them they were insane. She's come so far, and grown up so much in such a short space of time.

Somehow Tuwa looks much younger today. Perhaps it was the harshness of the fire light inside the cave, but her wrinkles do not seem so deep this morning. Arella looks around the glade. She cannot see anyone else in the area. The only people here are her and Tuwa. Everything looks so fresh. The rain from the night before has already gone. The only traces that water fell is the fresh smell in the grass. "Where is everyone?" Arella asks as she spiracles the old woman. She's decided that a polite approach will working better with her.

"There aren't many of us left child. But the women and children are not yet up, and the men have gone hunting." Tuwa explains.

"Do the women not hunt too?" Arella asks. This seems to be a common theme among the tribes and she thinks she knows the answer.

"Two do yes. But one is heavily pregnant at the moment and the other has a young child. They will not hunt until the children can be left with others." This is not the answer she was expecting, but it does not change the reason she has come to talk to Tuwa. "But this is not what you really came to ask me is it child?" This old lady is smarter than she seems.

"No it isn't." There's no point beat king around the bush. Tuwa knows Arella does not fully trust them.

"I don't have all day girl, ask what you wanted to ask so we can both get on with our day." Tuwa says.

"I wanted to know about Elsu's brother. What happened to him when he left the village?" Arella says.

"Is that the only question you have for me?" Tuwa pauses. "We'll then, I guess you should sit down. This is a long story and my neck will hurt if I have to look up at you for the whole thing." Arella takes a seat next to Tuwa and listens to her story.

"Wattan was a strange boy from the beginning. He and Elsu weren't just brothers, they were twins. They both learnt their abilities to shift into their animal forms young. Elsu found itch easier to shift from human to animal, and Wattan didn't like it. He grew very jealous of his brother. He believed that because he was the oldest, by an hour only, that he should be the one to find shifting easier." Tuwa begins. Arella is watching the expression on her face. It doesn't change the entire time the old woman speaks, she just stays calm, never showing emotion. "Both of them changed into the same creature. It was like nothing I've seen before. Like a giant raven."

"You're speaking as though it's in the past." Arella notices.

"That's because it is child." Tuwa explains. "Elsu no longer turns into the black bird. He decides the creature was too dangerous after what happened to his brother."

"What happened?" She pushes.

"If you let me speak I will tell you." Tuwa says. Arella is getting more involved in this story than she should be. She has almost forgotten the reason she wanted to hear about the brother. She pulls herself back into the present, remembering the reason for her interest.

"Wattan was becoming aggressive in his teenage years. This is common in skinwalkers, but most can learn either to suppress it or grow out of it. Others do not show any signs of aggression. But Wattan Struggled with it. He would snap at the smallest thing and was arguing with everyone. He found it very hard to control himself and was becoming a danger. More than once we had to separate him from the others."

"When he grew older, probably something close to your age, he left our tribe. It was around the time another group left." Tuwa pauses, clearly wondering whether to tell Arella the full story or not. "Let's just say we were having difficulties with some of the 'harder to handle' young ones. When he left, Elsu and a few of the others went looking for him. Here in the glade Wattan was safe. Even if he was a danger to us, we could control him. When he left us, he became a danger not only to himself but to others too."

"They searched for him for weeks, and they finally found him. By then it was too late. He'd come across a group of natives and killed one of them. They spotted him just as if happened but there was nothing they could do to stop it." Tuwa says, analysing Arella's face closely. She is careful bit to let anything slip, but she knew she was right. This means these people are dangerous, and they definitely shouldn't hang around here too long. After a pause Tuwa continues. "They followed Wattan for about a week after that until they managed to get close. Unfortunately they had to end his life. It was Elsu who did it. He's never really gotten over it."

"He killed his own brother?" Arella asks.

"He had no choice." Tuwa says. "How did you know Elsu had a brother anyway?"

"It was just a feeling. Something I overheard." Arella tries, but she knows the old woman does not believe her. "Thank you for telling me." Arella says. "Do you have any spare wood I could use to fix my bow?" She asks. She has to change subject, but it is true that she needs to fix her bow. It's broken, and she will no doubt need it on the way home. At least for hunting if nothing else. She pulls the how out from behind her back, revealing just how broken it is.

"There is a crop of those very same trees over there." Tuwa points towards a group of beautiful black trees. Arella has never seen these trees in such abundance. She is used to seeing just one or two, usually small or dying. But these are beautiful. Bright purple leaves sprout from the top of the tree, hanging down till they almost touch the ground.

"Thank you." Arella says again to the old woman. She then turns back to the cave where her friends are no doubt now awake, gets up from her place on the ground by the pond and starts walking back to them. She looks back as she walks and sees Tuwa staring at her. A very uneasy feeling washes over her, and Arella feels an urgency to leave this strange place.

When she gets back to the cave, she finds that the others are just waking up. All aside from Maska. He is already up, sharpening his claws on the sob eat the back of the cave. He purrs as Arella enters, acknowledging that she is there. "How long have you been up?" Nashoba asks.

"Just a while." Arella says, moving into his open arms and accepting the embrace. "You look much better today."

"I feel it." He smiles.

"When do you think you will be ready to travel?" Arella asks.

"Give him chance to rest." Nootau buts in. "He could do with the rest."

"It's okay Nootau. Arella's right. We need to get moving soon. I don't like it here. Something's not right."

"I'm going to go to that outcrop of trees over there and fix my bow. I want to be ready to leave under cover of darkness tonight." Arella says. "So rest up, eat up and be ready. I don't think getting out of here will be easy."

"We're not imprisoned Arella. I think we can leave whenever we want." Mato says.

"That's what they want you to think."

# Chapter 17

Arella and the others all head for the forest of anamoa trees. She looks around cautiously as they go, checking for any dangers that might be lurking in this unknown place. She really has no need to look for anything. Predators are not allowed in the glade, and hunting is limited to what people need to eat to survive. The people here mainly eat vegetables, roots, fruit and nuts, with the occasional meat if extra energy is needed.

There are a lot of anamoa trees in this area, and Arella has her pick of which one to use. She searches around the ground, looking for a suitable root to use. Roots she has found make the best material for bows as they are the right flexibility. The anamoa root is at any rate. After only a few minutes of searching she finds the perfect root. It is almost exactly the same as the one she used before, except this one is a little thicker and longer. The curve is just right, and as it is mostly out of the ground, it is not supporting the tree. "I'm going to use this one." Arella says, getting the attention of her friends.

"Awesome." Nashoba says. "Do you mind if I sit with you while you carve it? Nootau and Mato are going to do some fight training but I don't think I can join in yet." He gestures to his shoulder. The wound is still pink but you wouldn't know there was a spear in it just yesterday.

"I don't mind at all." Arella smiles.

Arella settles down on the ground with Nashoba beside her. He looks happy, content and not in pain for the first time in ages. It's nice to see him like this again. He's got the light back in his eyes. They are once again that bright mesmerising green Arella fell in love with. "What are you looking at?" He asks, catching her staring at him.

"You." Arella answers truthfully. "I can't stop thinking about how handsome you look."

"I don't think I've ever heard you say that." Nashoba admits. "Thank you." He's not quite sure how to take the compliment, and his cheeks turn a little red under the brown.

"I tell you what though." Arella smiles at him.

"What?" He asks.

"You really need a shave." Arella laughs. "It looks like there's a small mammal growing on your chin."

"You don't like it?" Nashoba toys with her, moving closer. He rubs his chin on Arella's face. "You sure you don't like it?"

"It's scratchy." She laughs, then Nashoba takes her face in his hands and kisses her. "I like that though." She smiles when he pulls away. They both go a little red now. Although they know they like each other, the feeling is still new and strange.

"Get a room you too!" Nootau shouts over from a short distance away. He and Mato are practicing their takedown skills. This is a familiar sight. Arella loves seeing the men like this. They've all grown up so much in such a short space of time. It's nice to see them playing again, having fun. She smiles, taking her dagger in her hand and behind carving at the root, making it the perfect size and shape to fire her arrows.

It feels natural to be carving the bow. She's done this before, and this time it's much much easier. Arella can't help but think that she should tell Nashoba about his father. After all, she knows the truth about the thing that killed him, and he does not. She looks over to him, he's just sitting there, watching Nootau and Mato fight, his fingers intertwined in Maska's fur. The auron cat purrs at his touch. He seems to be the only one who's come away from the whole ordeal with no injuries or harm done. But he's meant for this life, the travelling, the danger, the others aren't.

"Hey Nashoba, can we talk?" Arella asks. She's nervous all of a sudden. Why is she nervous? She has ok reason to be. This is not her secret to keep, and Nashoba deserves to know the truth about his father.

"Sure, what's up?" He smiles at her.

"It's about your father..." His expression changes instantly.

"What about him?" He says. Arella proceeds to tell him everything Tuwa told her about how Nashoba's father died. The entire time she was talking, Nashoba was silent. He just watched her face, his expression never changing. When she gets to the end he doesn't speak. He just sits in silence.

"Nashoba?" Arella breaks him out if the trance he seems to have fallen into.

"Hmm?"

"Are you okay?" She says gingerly.

"So you're telling me a skinwalker killed my father, and for no reason at all other than it couldn't control itself?"

"Yes, but it's okay. They killed him so he can't hurt anyone else." She says, hoping this will calm him. She can see Nashoba getting more and more angry. Perhaps it wasn't such a smart move to tell him this.

"Bastards!" Nashoba shouts.

"It's okay, he's gone now." Arella says. She glances over to Nootau and Mato who have noticed the irate Nashoba.

"What's wrong?" Nootau asks.

"Arella's just told me a bloody skinwalker killed my father. I'm mad."

He says, although some of the anger is dissipating now. Perhaps this is not the right time to tell him that she might be the daughter of a skinwalker.

Arella continues to carve her bow out, leaving Nashoba to stew in his anger. He will calm down again soon. After all, he's just found out who killed his father. Silence falls over the two of them, and Nootau and Mato go back to their practice.

"It should have been me." Nashoba says out of the blue, making Arella jump. She cuts her hand on the dagger, just a little blood but a lot of pain.

"What should have been you?" She asks.

"It should have been me to kill the skinwalker." He says. Arella looks up from her bow to see tears in his eyes. "If I was there... If I was with him..." His voice breaks off. Arella goes to him to comfort him.

"It's not your fault Nashoba. There's nothing you could have done." She says.

"I would have killed it." He looks at Arella's face, calm and together. "We definitely can't stay here with these people. We're getting out of here as soon as we can." He says

"I agree." Arella says. "But I think we have to do it under cover of darkness." She smiles. "Besides, I want to finish this how before we go." Nashoba looks down at the bow in Arella's lap.

"Looks almost finished to me." He says.

"Oh it is." She says.

The sun has started to set, and Kuruk and Migisi are back from their days hunting. They've brought back a boar for the village to eat. This is the first time Arella and the others have seen the rest of the villagers. There are are so many of them too. Some with white skin and pale hair, others with dark red skin and black hair, then there are those in between. There are children too. Maybe a dozen of them, it's hard to count when they're all tuning around. They all sit around a fire near the cave Nashoba was treated in, the boar roasting over it. People are enjoying a multitude of fruits and nuts. If Arella hadn't been out in the snow just a couple of days ago she would have completely forgotten it was winter. Back home will by now have snow. Arella thinks of her home and how beautiful it looks in winter.

Arella looks over at Nashoba. "I don't want to join them." He says quietly.
"Me either but we have to keep up appearances." Arella answers.
"Don't worry, we'll be out of here soon enough." She takes his hand, and together with Nootau, Mato and Maska, they joking the group of strange skinwalkers.

It's strange to look at these people. In a way it is what Arella would like. People getting on with each other even though they are all different. Some of the people here are clearly skinwalkers they have the traits of the animals they turn into. While others may not be. Kuruk is sitting at the head of the fire and the sky is darkening, orange perking over the clouds and stars beginning to shine in the sky.

"Have I told the story of how skinwalkers got their skins recently?" Kuruk asks. The children all laugh with joy. This is clearly a story they enjoy. Arella can't help thinking this seems very much like when the skinwalkers that captured them further down the mountains were telling stories. Although she doesn't think that this one will end with them being the meal. "Well then, let's begin." He smiles. The children all get comfortable and quieter down as Kuruk begins telling his story.

"It started hundreds of years ago. My great grandfather told me this story, as his grandfather told him, and someday I will tell my grandchildren." Arella notices he looks at her but she doesn't think anyone rose notices. "This story goes all the way back to when our tribe lived on the ground, in the forests far below this mountain. We were like any other tribe. We followed the same laws, hunted, built huts and survived, but there was one thing that set us apart from the other tribes. Does anybody know what that was?" He asks. Lots of little hands fly into the air, children eager to please. Kuruk nods to one child, a head of long dark hair gives her answer in a squeaky female tone.

"It was the chiefs love of nature."

"We'll remembered." Kuruk continues. "Some of the other tribes thought they were put here just to kill and that all animals should bow to them, but our chief was different. He knew that the animals lives were sacred and that they should be protected. He made the whole village promise that they would only kill when they needed to eat or when the animal was in need of having its life ended."

"The villagers lived in peace with nature for years, and as a result, the village prospered. There was no sickness in the tribe, and they were thriving in the forest. Some of the villagers even took the animals as their pets. Most of these villagers were warriors, and as such took predators as companions. Wolves, eagles and hunting dogs were common in the village, but they did not attack the villagers of the livestock they kept."

"The villagers had seen a spirit in the mountains above the forest where they lived. Does anyone know which animal this spirit took the shape of?" Kuruk asks the group of children.

"A bear!" They all shout in unison.

"That's right, a bear. The villagers learned from this bear, watching it hunt in the river that flowed from the mountain, watching it eat not only meat but other things too, living off the land but never destroying it. They began to worship the spirit bear. In autumn, the bear travelled up the mountain to hibernate. The villagers all knew this. One year, a group of the warriors, all young men with inquisitive minds, decided that they would follow the bear to see where it went. They knew it travelled up the mountain every autumn, then returned again in spring, but they did not know what it did while it was up there, or even what was at the top of the mountain."

"The young men followed the bear up the mountain, and what they found was a shock to all of them. They found the glade. Not only was it strange to see that there were things growing this high up, but they had passed through snow and biting cold all the way up the mountain, only to find that the glade was warm and full of animals. The animal in the centre of the glade was the bear. The young men saw the spirit bear turn into a man before their very eyes. They were all shocked, and a little frightened. The spirit man walked towards the men and began speaking to them." Kuruk then took on the voice of the spirit. He started talking in a deep voice. "Why have you followed me up the mountain?" The children all gasp as though this is the first time they have heard the story. "The men all tried to speak, but they were too frightened. One young man stepped forwards to talk. *"We followed you to see where you went. But you were a bear. How are you now a man?"* The spirit was surprised that one of the men spoke to him with such confidence. *"I am the mountain spirit, and I have power over all nature around here. I can turn into whichever animal I please."* The men on the mountain couldn't understand this. It was unbelievable to the, The brave young man spoke again. *"Why do you always stay close to our village?"*

The mountain spirit considered his response, then spoke. *"I have been watching your village for a long time, and I have come to a conclusion. I am going to grant you the same powers I have myself, in return you must do something for me... You must bring your village to the glade and live here. Keep it protected, and someday I will return. I have to attend to other parts of this world. They need me."* The young men were excited and accepted the mountain spirit's request." The children all laugh and giggle among themselves. "From then on, the people of out tribe have been able to skinwalk." Kuruk finished his story. Arella can't help but that how beautiful it was.

The group sit around eating for the next hour or so until the sun has gone completely and the only light is now moon, stars and the dying fire. Most people have now gone to be, but a few people are still sitting around talking. Arella looks over to Nashoba. "I think we should all go to bed now." She says.

"I'm knackered." Nootau yawns.

"Me too. Sleep sounds like a good idea." Mato says.

"Yeah okay. Let's go." Nashoba says. He gets up from the ground and offers Arella his hand. She takes it, and the four of them begin walking away from the fire towards the cave they slept in the night before.

Nashoba, Nootau and Mato all lie down on the ground, covered by furs. It doesn't take long for them to fall asleep. Arella however has stayed awake. Her and Maska are watching for everyone else in this tribe to fall asleep. Once the coast is clear, she will wake the others so they can leave. Arella feels a little bad about this, leaving in the middle of the night without even a goodbye, but something just doesn't feel right about this place.

It doesn't take long until it looks like everyone is asleep. Arella gets up from her seated position on the ground and leaves the cave. She has a look around, then stands still and listens. Nothing She calls Maska to her side. "Can you hear anyone?" She asks him. He just blinks at her then purrs. This means he cannot hear anyone else either. "Let's get them up then." She says. Her and Maska enter the cave again, this time to wake up the men. She goes to wake Nashoba first, who awakens slightly groggy, but in a good mood. Arella is nervous, and by the time she has finished waking Nashoba, Nootau and Mato have already been awoken by Maska. "Collect all of your things, and let's go." Arella says. They do this, and everyone is ready within less than a minute.

Arella leads them towards the gate. It's closed when they reach it, but there's no one guarding it. "There's no one here." Mato whispers as he walks towards the gate.

"Don't touch it." Nootau rushes, remembering what happened to him when he touched it last time. Arella steps forwards towards it. She can feel the energy pulsing from it.

"What are you doing?" A voice says from behind. They all jump. Arella turns to see Kuruk and Migisi standing behind them.

"Leaving." Arella says. "Thank you for your help, but we're going home now."

"You can't leave." Kuruk says.

"And why not?" Arella asks.

"Because you came here for a reason." Migisi says.

"We came here to have Nootau healed. We have done that, and now we can go home." Arella says.

"Except that's not the reason you came here is it?" Kuruk says.

"The reason is irreverent. We want to go home and you can't

keep us here." Nashoba says.

"Where is home?" Migisi asks.

"Home is home. It's none of your business where we live." Nootau says.

"But why did you come here if you just want to go home? Why did you leave your home in the first place?" Kuruk pushes.

"Eugh." Arella is getting sick of this. They're not going to get out of this easy, and she's going to have to end this quickly before the rest of the village wake up. "We came here for me." She says. "They came here to find answers to who I am. But that doesn't matter anymore. I know who I am, and I want to go home."

"You are home." Kuruk says.

"What's he saying?" Nootau asks.

"Arella, stay here. This is your true home." Kuruk pushes.

"Arella what does he mean?" Mato asks. This is going too far. Arella feels hot, she feels sick, but most of all she feels angry.

"I'm his daughter. That's what he's saying. They think I'm a skinwalker and I should stay here with them. But that's bull..." Arella shouts.

"You know it's true." Kuruk says. "You look like me. And you control that beast just like a skinwalker."

"I do not control Maska." Arella is irate. "And I am not a skinwalker!" She storms towards the gate and smashes her closed fists against it. A flash of bright purple light fills the sky, but the gates open.

"Only a skinwalker can open that gate." Migisi says. The men stare at Arella, all of them except Nashoba. Arella storms through the gate. Nootau, Mato, Maska and Nashoba follow her through, but Migisi and Kuruk stay within the glade.

"You always have a home here Arella. Just you wait till they kick you out again. Wait until they shun you from being different." Kuruk says as they walk away. Hot tears threaten in Arella's eyes. She breaks out into a run, letting the tears fall from her face. "You'll be back!"

# Chapter 18

Arella runs until her lungs are burning, until she can't run anymore. The gripping pain in her chest was becoming too much and the tears were there again. She collapses to the ground. Everything has gotten way too real, way too fast and she's struggling to cope with it. She's just found out a lot about herself, and now the others know too. She hits the ground hard, and doesn't get up. Arella doesn't want to get up. She wants the ground to swollen her whole and never let her go. Darkness surrounds her in more than one way. In the black of the night, lot only by the light of the moon and stars, Arella lies on the ground near the waterfall. A sudden blackness envelopes her, and Arella goes unconscious. As she is going under, she's aware of voices shouting her name. She does not answer. She cannot answer. The darkness takes her once again.

"Why did she run off like that?" Nootau asks, out of breath and panting from running.

"We have to catch up to her, it's too dark to be running up here. She might fall off the mountain." Nashoba says. He too is out of breath, and his chest it hurting a little. He shouldn't be doing strenuous exercise yet. The wound has not fully healed, and although the process has been sped up, it will still be a couple of days before he can act as normal. Nashoba knows this is bad for him, but they have to get to Arella before she hurts herself. She's upset, and rightly so, but they have to find her.

It feels like they've been running forever. "Gods that girl can run." Mato breathes as the waterfall comes into view.

"There she is." Nashoba says. Maska is standing close by, watching over her. She's still unconscious when they get to her. "What happened?" Nashoba says, scooping her up into his arms and moving her.

"Looks like she fainted." Nootau says, catching his breath. "I'd assume from the adrenalin and shock."

"I'll get our things." Mato says. "We might need the furs for sleeping further down the mountain." Nashoba looks questioningly at him.

"Oh I forgot, you were pretty out of it by this point. We left our bags here. It was becoming to much to carry with having to help you walk as well, and it was getting warmer too. But I think we'll need then soon." He collects the bags they were hidden, still where they stashed them, untouched.

Arella's eyes flutter open. "Hey beautiful." Nashoba says to her.

"How can you call me that?" She says, tears already forming in her eyes.

"And here was me thinking beautiful was a compliment." He laughs. "What's wrong?"

"I'm a skinwalker. You heard them." One of the tears falls. Nashoba brushes it away with a soft hand. Arella looks around, seeing all the people she considers friends. "I'm a skinwalker."

"So what?" Nootau says. This is not the reaction she was expecting.

"What do you mean so what?" Arella is outraged. These men should be disgusted with her, they should be repulsed by the very sight of her. "I'm a monster." Another tear falls.

"You are not a monster." Nashoba says, looking her in the eyes. Arella stares back at his. Dark emerald green. There is no hint of a lie, nor any anger in his eyes. He really doesn't care that she's a skinwalker. She looks around at all of them, none of them care.

"Okay so you might be a skinwalker." Nootau says.

"But you're our skinwalker." Mato laughs. Arella lets out a small laugh too, her tears drying in her eyes. They accept her, for all she is.

"Now let's get out of here and go home." Nashoba smiles. "All if us."

The journey home seems much easier than their journey up the mountain. Perhaps it's because they're finally going home, or maybe it's because they all feel lighter, no more worries, no more questions. Or maybe it's just because they are going down hill all the way back.

They pass the place where the crows attacked them first. They take their time on these cliffs, careful not to fall. Next, they come across the cave where they took temporary shelter once Nashoba had been stabbed by the spear, before the bear that turned out to be Arella's father attacked them.

They continue their journey back down the mountain, all feeling stronger and happier the further down they go. They half expected it to get warmer too, bit are quickly reminded that it is now winter all around. This does not dampen their spirits though.

They spent their time on the way back how they thought it would be on the way there. They had no trouble with predators or skinwalkers. They did not see a single other person or threat the whole way back. They spent the time talking, hunting for food, sitting by campfires and telling stories. It was absolute bliss, but none of them wanted anymore more than to be home.

On the sixth day of the journey back, the group find themselves on a patch of clear ground, covered in a thick layer of snow. This land is next to the lake. Arella can see the forest she calls home across the water. It's so close now. She looks across the frozen lake. It maybe only two days walk away. They could be there tomorrow if they could cross the lake. They'll have to stay here tonight. The sun is already on its way down. Suddenly, something hard and cold hits her on the back of the neck. She turns quickly, the cold ice dripping down the back of her neck. "Who was that?" She says, laughing. "And what the hell was it?"

"A snowball." Nootau laughs. Arella bends to the ground and scoops snow into her hand. She balls it up and launches it at him, hitting him square in the chest. "Her, it was Nashoba, not me."

"It was not me. Don't like Nootau." Nashoba laughs.

"It so was you." Mato joins in. Arella bends to the ground and scoops up more snow, but she's too slow. Nashoba hits her with a snowball. She now knows it was him that threw first. The ball hits with the same power as the one before. Once she has recovered from the attack, Arella throws her ball at him. It hits its mark. The others soon join in, and Maska runs for cover. He doesn't much like the cold, and he's not really enjoying the snow anyway.

After half an hour of playing in the snow, they all have numb hands. The orange of the sun is glowing in the sky, the sun it setting and they haven't built a fire or shelter yet. "I think we need to get serious now guys." Arella laughs. "I hate to break up this fun, but my hands are freezing, and it's going to get pretty cold out here soon if we don't make a shelter."

"Yeah, you're right." Nashoba says, taking charge of the situation. This used to bother Arella a little, but she no longer cares. All she wants is to be back home, to now be spending her entire day walking, to be able to relax properly.

They focus on the fire. They have been harder to make recently, the snow making everything wet. But they have become good at making fires in any weather. This is the most important part of keeping them warm tonight. The second thing they made was a shelter. This would simply keep the snow off them if it came in the night. It does not seem as though this will happen though, the sky is clear again tonight. "This could be our last night out here guys." Arella says as she places a hare over the flames to cook. They'd caught a few earlier in the day and kept them until now for cooking.

"I thought we'd still be a couple of days away at least." Nashoba says.

"I figure, well I was trying to work it out anyway before someone threw a snowball at me..." Arella shoots a look at Nashoba. He just stifles a smile. "That we could cross the lake." The men stare at her in disbelief.

"How could we cross the lake. It would be freezing, and that's if we could even break the... Oh." Nashoba gets it.

"We walk over the ice" Arella announces. "I was trying to work out if it would be thick enough, then ice hit the back of my head and I was sidetracked." She smiles. "I think it will be though. That would cut a day or more out of our travel time. We could be back at your village by tomorrow night."

"Our village." Nashoba says.

"It's not my village though." Arella sighs. "I don't live there."

"No, but you can if you want to." Nashoba smiles. "We want you to, don't we boys?"

"Yeah."

"Of course we do." They say.

"But what about the others?" Arella asks.

"Stuff the others." Nashoba smiles. "I'll be chief when we get home, and they will listen to me. There is nothing so different about you, aside from your skin and hair, and nothing wrong with you at all. They will just have to grow up and stop being afraid of things they don't understand."

"Thank you guys." Arella smiles. "Hey, there's one thing I didn't tell you that I found out from the skinwalkers."

"What's that?"

"I'm the granddaughter of a chief." She says.

"You're what?" The men all chorus in unison.

"Yeah. I overheard Kuruk saying that my mother was the daughter of the chief at the time. He disowned her when he found out my mother was pregnant with me. Then her brother took over the tribe. This is why they never killed me or shut me out completely, because I was the chief's niece." She says. That's everything she's needed to tell them. She now has everything off her chest, and feels a whole lot lighter.

The sky is bright blue the next morning. "A beautiful morning." Arella says with a giant smile on her face as she wakes up. She's going home today, and she couldn't be happier.

"A beautiful morning to wake up next to a beautiful girl." Nashoba says next to her.

"You don't look so bad yourself Mr." Arella says.

"I think I'm going to throw up last night's hare." Nootau says, making retching noises.

"Ah, get over it Nootau. We all know you're the soppiest person on the planet when you've fallen for someone." Mato laughs. "I think it's sweet. Nashoba's never liked anyone like he likes Arella. It's clear just from looking at them together. When you find someone like that, you'll be worse by far."

"I guess. But still." Nootau laughs. "Are we going to get going then? I want my own bed back."

"Yeah. Everyone up and at it then." Nashoba says.


Arella heads straight for the lake with Maska hot on her heels. He's the lightest, followed by her. "Maska?" Arella says, getting his attention. He looks up at her with his odd coloured eyes. "Do you want to do something stupid and probably incredibly dangerous?" The auron cat blinks at her and nods. "Let's go then." She looks back at the men who are just behind her. "We're going to go first, check if the ice is thick enough. If we can walk on it together, you guys should have no problems walking single file."

"Are you sure this is a good idea?" Mato asks. He's the biggest, and is not as much of a strong swimmer as the others. He's nervous, and it's understandable.

"It will be fine Mato. Don't worry." She reassures him. "And this way we get home quicker too."

"I guess." He agrees.


Arella takes a tentative step out onto the icy lake. The ground beneath her feet is slippery, but solid. She takes a few more steps, and Maska stays close by her side. Both of them move slowly, but the ice is holding beneath their weight. She can see the other side. They can make is across in less than an hour from here, then it will only be a couple of hours till they get to the village. "I think it's okay to start coming across." She says when she is about twenty feet onto the giant ice sheet. Nashoba is next on the ice. He slips a little with his first steps, but manages to steady himself enough to carry on walking. Nootau follows close behind, and although Mato is hesitant, he too steps onto the ice to walk across.


They all make it to the other side with no problems. Arella is relieved when her feet back back on solid ground. She lets out an audible sigh, and turns to see the others also coming to the end of the ice and stepping onto the hard ground she is standing on. Mato is the happiest to be off the ice. "I'm so glad we made it over." He sighs. "That would have ended badly if one of us had fallen through."

"Good job you've lost some weight then Mato." Nootau laughs.

"Hey!" Mato shoves his arm, making his a little off balance. He falls on his bum, landing in the snow.

"Now, now children." Arella says. "Let's get going."

The rest of the walk back to the village is easy, and it doesn't take long until they can hear the voices of the villagers. "I've missed those sounds." Nootau says.

"Me too. Oh I can't wait to get into my own bed tonight." Mato says.

"And some good food." Nootau breathes in. "Not that your cooking isn't good Arella, but there's nothing better than your mothers own cooking."

"Your mum's cooking is the best." Mato agrees. "She has a way with food that's just mouthwatering, wait till you taste it." Mato stops talking. Nashoba and Arella have stopped walking up ahead.

"What's wrong?" Nashoba asks Arella.

"I'm nervous." She says. "When you left your village, Nova was trying to kill me, and Doahte was with her. What if the village have rallied behind them?"

"It will be fine Arella. They will all follow me. Now come on. Let's go into the village. Let's go home." Together they all leave the edge of the forest, entering the village.

# Chapter 19

The whole village are staring at the group as they walk in from the clearing. Every single eye watching them as they walk. Nashoba looks at Arella. She looks so nervous. He's not ever seen her look this scared. Not with the hunting hounds, nor the beast they came across in the forest. Not with the skinwalkers, or the bear. He has never seen her look so scared. She is physically shaking. He didn't realise how much of a big deal this would be to her. To him and the others they are simply going home, but this is so much more to Arella, and she is frightened. He takes her hand in his, and they walk to wards the centre of the village. This act in itself causes sharp inhales from some, and whispers from others, but Nashoba ignores them.

"Well, well, well. Look who is it." A female voice says from behind. It's Nova. Of course it's her. Who else would it be. "I see you decided to come back big brother."

"Of course I came back." He says. "We all came back."

"And you brought that thing with you too." She sneers. Maska growls at her. Arella holds her hand up, and he backs off. "And I didn't mean the cat." She looks Arella up and down.

"She's with me." Nashoba says. Nova glances down at their intertwined hands.

"You can't tell me this is true." She laughs. "You and that thing are together? Don't make me laugh."

"She's not a thing Nova. She's a beautiful person, and I love her." Nashoba says.

"You love her? You wouldn't know the meaning of love." Nova starts.

"I've had enough of this." Doahte pipes up.

"Oh I might have known you'd be hanging around her still." Nootau says.

"And what's that supposed to mean?" Doahte asks.

"Just what I said. You're like a fly Doahte." Nootau says.

"Why a fly?"

"Always hanging around sh..."

"Enough the both of you." Nashoba says. "This is getting too much. Nova, just stand down."

"You disappeared for weeks Nashoba, without telling anyone where you were going." Nova says. "You left us, and now you're expecting just to come straight back in and take over?"

"It's my right to be in charge of this tribe Nova." Nashoba says.

"You lost that right when you left the tribe with her." She spits. Arella is hurt, but so is Nashoba. She looks up at him. All she sees on his face in anger, pure hatred for his own sister.

"Enough children." Ujarak says. "This is no way to treat each other. You're siblings. You shouldn't be fighting like this."

"Shut up old man!" Doahte shouts at him.

"Hey. Did no one ever teach you to respect your elders?" Arella is mad now. Ujurak was just trying to help. There was no need for Doahte to go off on him like that.

"And you can shut up too!" He raises a how to Arella. "Shut up or I shoot this arrow right at your heart." The whole tribe erupts into gasps and whispers.

"Whoa, just calm down Doahte." Nootau tries to reason with him.

"No I won't calm down!" He shouts. "Everything was perfect when you weren't here. Now you're back and you're going to ruin everything!" The anger is taking over him. Everything seems to move in slow motion. Arella looks at each person is turn. They all look scared. Clearly Doahte has never done something like this, and none of them know if he will go through with it or not. She steps forwards, taking her hand from Nashoba's. Maybe if she can talk with Doahte, tell him she will leave and not come back, maybe he will lower his bow. Nashoba tries to hold her hand, to hold her back, but his hand is sweaty with nerves and hers slips out.

"Just stop there. Don't go any further." Arella can see Doahte is shaking. She lifts up her hands in a gesture of surrender.

"Don't do anything stupid Doahte. Just listen for a minute please." She tries to reason with him. His arms are shaking, and it doesn't look like he's going to be able to hold the bow taught for another second. In slow motion, the arrow comes loose from the bow and fires towards Arella. She inhales sharply and closes her eyes, waiting for impact, but she does not feel any pain.


Gasps and cries fill the air, and Arella opens her eyes. What she sees will stay with her for her entire life. On the floor in front of her, with the arrow that was meant for her, is Ujarak. The old man had jumped in front of Arella, sacrificing himself for her. He is bleeding profusely. Arella is first at him body on the ground. She puts her hands on the wound on his chest, blood pumping from it at an alarming rate. She presses her hands against his chest, trying to stop the pain. "Nootau!" She shouts. The young healer comes to her side.

"I...I... I don't know what to do." He stutters.

"We have to do something. If we don't he's going to..." Arella is becoming emotional.

"Arella, stop." Ujarak's wheezy voice says. "It's too late."

"No." Tears are forming in Arella's eyes. Others from the tribe are already crying. They know the arrow is too much for the old man. Even if he was young and healthy, the wound would be too much for him. The arrow has hit him directly in the heart, and it's only a mater of minutes before he bleeds out. "You can't die." Arella is crying now. "You can't." She didn't realise how much this old man had meant to her. She barely knew him, but he was good to her, and he sacrificed his own life to save her.

"Promise me something Arella." He coughs, blood coming from his mouth as he does so. Arella takes her sleeve and wipes it from his face.

"Anything Ujarak." She whispers.

"Be good to Nashoba. He needs you more than you could imagine. They all do." He coughs again, then goes still. The old man has breathed his last breath.

Arella looks up from the body of the man who saved her life, to the one who intended to end it. Doahte looks devastated. He looks from his hand with the bow in it, to Ujarak on the ground, then back to his hand. He drops the bow on the ground. "What have I done?" He says to himself.

"Doahte." Nashoba says. There are tears in his eyes, but he has a job to do. He is chief of this tribe, and he has to punish Doahte and Nova for what they've done. Doahte looks at him. "What you have done..." Nashoba doesn't know what to say. Arella wants to help, but this isn't her place. Instead she helps Nootau and Mato with moving Ujarak's body. They will take it to the field where his body will be burried like the other warriors in the tribe for that is what he was. "You cannot stay in this tribe any longer. The penatly for killing one of our own is death."

"You can't kill him." Nova pipes up.

"I could." Nashoba says angrily. "I have every right to. But I'm not going to do that." Doahte looks relieved. "Instead I'm going to banish the both of you."

"But Nashoba..." Nova tries.

"I won't hear anymore of it." Nashoba looks away from her and towards Ujarak who is bieng carried away. "You have until the sun goes down to get out of the village. If I ever see either of you here again, I will have you both killed." Nashoba leaves them there, with all the eyes of the village staring at them, and goes to pay his respects to a lost friend.

# Epilogue

A pale skinned white haired woman sits on the ground surrounded by spring flowers in the meadow. She's braiding her hair, placing a blue feather in it, and tying it with a leather strap at the bottom. Her auron cat is off hunting, bringing back something special for dinner. It's been three years since Arella was accepted into the tribe, and today is a very special day. A short distance away, a beautiful green eyed, white haired girl, with tanned skin is playing with her daddy. She turns one today. Her laughter fills the air. A light airy laugh that would bring a smile to anyone's face. She cannot speak yet, but her eyes tell a thousand words.

"Let's go get your Mummy." A familiar voice says. Arella see's them coming through the long grass and pretty flowers. Both with bright green eyes, both hers. Nashoba and their daughter Taini. Her white hair bounces as she runs towards her mother, a big smile on her pretty face, her arms extended. Arella welcomes her into them, then takes Nashoba into them aswell. "I love you my white ghost." He says to her.

"And I love you, my red wolf." Arella says back. "Forever and always."


The End!

Follow @SteeleKellie for new releases.


https://www.facebook.com/KellieSteeleWriting/


Coming soon…..


Chronicals of Araxx – The Beginning

# Chronicles of

# Araxx

# The Beginning

## Prologue

The alarms were blaring loud, red lights flashing and blinding in the warehouse. A gunshot flew right last Lee's face as she hid around the corner. "Since when did werewolves have the need for firearms!?" She shouted over the chaos.

"You have a lot to learn." Ads laughed. "Werewolves don't use guns, but their familiars do."

"They're panicking!" Jay shouted from the other side of the warehouse. Shielded behind one of the large crates, alone with another Lee did not recognise.

"You would be too if we were coming for you." Ads yelled back to him. He and Lee were sheltered behind another set of crates. Gunfire bounced off the wall behind them, chips of brick coming loose and falling to the ground, the sound almost deafening.

"We have to get out of here!" One of the familiars firing guns shouted to his companions.

"We can take 'em. They're just a bunch of kids!" Another yelled.

"They're agents of the Araxx!" The first man yelled through a break in gunfire.

"Agents? I like that!" Lee Smiled.

"Yeah, we've not been called that before. I'm taking that one!" Jay called back.

"We're here to do a job." The lieutenant called over. "I knew you weren't ready for this mission, but the colonel believes in children apparently. Don't prove him wrong!"

"You heard him boys! We've got a job to do, so let's grab that bastard and get it over with." Lee yelled. She stood from her position behind the crate, took aim on one of the familiars hiding at the other side of the room and fired. The gun shot rang out as it fired from the 9mm pistol, flying at great speed towards its target.

A cry of pain came from the man as the bullet lodged itself in his leg.

"You missed his head." Jay laughed, taking aim on another one if the familiars, taking him out with ease.

"Completely intended dear Jay. Don't kill that one, he's mine." Lee too aim on another man, this time the shot from her gun landing itself in his skull, penetrating his helmet with ease.

It was clear these men were unprepared for the attack. They were wearing green camouflage clothing, but with simple stab prof vests and helmets. Although they all held guns, none of these men were a decent shot. There were a dozen of the at the beginning. A dozen familiars, against four members of the Araxx, three of them only teenagers on their first mission. By the end of the fight, there were only the four, and the familiar Lee left alive.

"You wanted this one keeping alive Lee?" Ads asked her, looking back over his shoulder as he stood in front of the familiar with the bullet wound deep in his thigh.

"I have questions for him." Lee answered as she strode over to her prisoner, emptying the clip on her gun as she went. She snapped a new one into place just as she came to him. "This one I recognise."

"Annaleah Hemplesworth." The man laughed. "I might have known you'd come back to us eventually."

"Where is Logan?" Lee ignored what the man first said, pushing her question forwards instead.

"And why would I tell you that bitch?" He spat at her. Lee raised her gun to his stomach. The man laughed in her face from the ground where he sat, blood pooled around his from his leg. "You won't shoot me, you need answers." He said confidently. Lee pulled the trigger, the bullet finding itself in the mans shoulder.

"Oh trust me I will shoot you." Lee smiled at him. She enjoyed her revenge just a little too much. "Now tell me where he is."

"I'm not telling you anything." He said again, this time through gritted teeth from the pain. Lee again emptied another bullet into the man, this one landed in his other leg. The man yelled out in pain.

"I'm asking you one more time. Now answer me."

"Last we was he was in London. But he wouldn't tell us where he was staying." He finally gave in, the pain becoming too much. The man feared for his life.

"Thank you." She said as she turned away. "Oh and it's Lee now." She finished as she shot another bullet, this one entered the familiars head, punctured his brain and came out the other side. He slumped to the floor, dead.

19555259R00134

Printed in Great Britain
by Amazon